I ran in slow motion, like someone in a nightmare with nightmare creatures snapping at their heels. But this wasn't a bad dream, and the creatures weren't imaginary. They were real. And they were deadly.

I'm dead! I thought, with every crunching, sliding, heart-stopping step.

I knew the risk I was facing. All it would take was a single scorpion to get flicked up onto my calf and sting me through my jeans, and I'd be cactus ...

EXTREME ADVENTURES

BOOK 4

JUSTIN D'ATH

A DIVISION OF EDC PUBLISHING

First American Edition 2010
Kane Miller, A Division of EDC Publishing
Revised cover, 2013

First published in 2006 by Penguin Group (Australia)
Text copyright © Justin D'Ath 2006

Library of Congress Control Number: 2009943489

Printed and bound in the United States of America
1 2 3 4 5 6 7 8 9 10
ISBN: 978-1-61067-220-7

For Rachael

DINOSAUR

Nathan led the way. It felt like we were the last two people alive in a black, silent world. We both wore helmets. A thirteen-foot safety rope connected us, in case one of us slipped. The floor was rocky and uneven. In a couple of places we had to climb down nearly vertical shafts. It was slow going. My big brother was an experienced caver, but he was being extra careful because no human being had ever set foot in here before. Anything could be around the next corner.

About a third of a mile from the cave entrance, we came to a rock fall. Nathan wormed his way over, then turned back to help me. As I wriggled across the chest-high pile of rubble, I glimpsed something over Nathan's shoulder.

No way! I thought.

I was so busy gawking that I lost my balance and fell on top of him. We tumbled down the rock pile, our flashlight beams slashing like lightsabers through the dust cloud kicked up by our sliding bodies. When we came to rest, I was lying on my back, looking up at an enormous, grinning skull.

"A T-rex!" I gasped.

"I don't think so," said Nathan. He helped me to my feet. "Look at the teeth. It's an herbivore."

I didn't argue. Nathan is a tour guide for an outback adventure company. He's an expert on everything to do with the outdoors and wildlife – even wildlife that's been dead for millions of years.

"Do you have any idea what kind it is?" I asked.

Nathan chuckled. "You don't need to whisper, Sam – it won't hear you." He moved his flashlight beam across the scatter of large brown bones partially embedded in the cave wall and ceiling. "I'd say it's an ancestor of the kangaroo. A super 'roo. Look at the size of that femur. It must have stood twenty feet tall."

"Wow," I said. "Imagine how high it could jump!"

Nathan rummaged through his backpack for his digital camera. "I'll get some pictures," he said. "I know a guy at the Sydney museum who's going to do backflips when he finds out about this."

I grinned to myself. When Nathan mentioned he'd discovered a hidden cave mouth during a desert safari three weeks earlier, it had been my idea to come back and explore it. Nathan hadn't been keen – it was a very long drive, and we were in the middle of a heatwave – but I'd kept at him until he agreed. So it was mostly thanks to me that we'd discovered the prehistoric kangaroo.

"Can you get a photo of me?" I asked.

"I've got heaps of photos of you, bro," Nathan said.

"With the dinosaur."

"Fair enough. Stand next to the head and put your hand on its jaw." He looked through the viewfinder. "Say cheese."

"Cheese," I said, and the camera flashed.

There was a rumble.

The floor shook.

Then the entire cave roof collapsed on top of us.

2

I KILLED MY BROTHER!

It was my fault. I hadn't expected the flash to be so bright. We had been underground for nearly an hour, and my eyes had become accustomed to the gloom. When Nathan clicked his camera, it was like a magnesium flare going off in my face. I must have flinched and accidentally leaned on the dinosaur's jaw. The ancient bone hadn't been touched for a million years, much less *leaned* on. It cracked. Which started a chain reaction. A whole series of cracks went shooting up through the other bones and spread across the cave's ceiling like a giant spider's web.

Then it all came crashing down.

I was knocked to the ground by the cave-in. But I

was lucky – one of the massive thigh bones fell diagonally across me. It was stronger than the others and didn't shatter. It formed a sloping girder, protecting me from the other falling bones and clay and rock. Nathan had made me wear my old bicycle helmet, so I didn't get brained. Apart from a few bumps and grazes, I felt okay.

My flashlight was lying next to my elbow, its beam turned a dull orange by all the dust in the air. I grabbed it and looked around. There was a small gap behind me. I managed to wriggle out, legs first, then struggled carefully to my feet.

The cave looked different in the settling dust. The ceiling was much higher than it had been, and a huge mound of bones and rubble rose up in the center of the floor. Trailing out of the mound, one end tied around my waist, was the rope.

"Nathan?" I whispered.

Silence.

"Nathan!" I crouched over the rope where it disappeared under the rocks. I gave it a gentle tug, but the rope was stuck. My brother was at the other end. With several tons of rubble lying on top of him.

I'd killed my brother!

I set the flashlight on a small boulder and began digging. I tore away rocks, pieces of bone, lumps of dirt. Inch by inch, I uncovered the rope. It was dusty, tattered and frayed. In one place, a bone shard had cut it almost in two. I tried not to imagine what the cave-in had done to my brother. Gritting my teeth, I concentrated on digging.

Five minutes later, I rolled aside a heavy slab of rock. And there was Nathan's camera. Pulverized. Dreading what I was about to find, I lifted another rock.

My whole world seemed to stop. A hand lay in the rubble. It wasn't moving. A worm of red blood curled around the base of one fingernail. Dust clung to the dark hairs below the knuckles. I drew back, unable to touch it. I knew that hand almost as well as my own. How many times in the last fourteen years had it grasped mine? Or fixed a bike tire for me? Or untangled a fishing line? Fifteen minutes ago, it had helped me across the first rock fall.

It seemed impossible that Nathan was dead. He was nine years older than me, and all my life I'd looked up to him. He was my big brother, my best friend. I'd always thought he was indestructible.

I was trembling all over. It was difficult to breathe. Tears blurred my vision as I built up the courage to reach forward and touch my dead brother's hand.

One of his fingers ... moved!

Then they all did. Moving like the tentacles of a waking octopus, Nathan's fingers wrapped slowly around my hand and gave it a gentle squeeze.

3

STRETCHER CASE

It took about ten minutes to dig Nathan out. He hadn't been as lucky as me. His lightweight caving helmet had stopped his head from being crushed, but no giant kangaroo bone had fallen over him and formed a protective bridge. He had a broken arm, a broken leg, and he reckoned several ribs were cracked too.

"You'll have to get help," he croaked.

"I'm not leaving you here," I said, crouching over him. "I'll carry you out."

He gave me a weak smile in the dim orange light. His teeth were chattering. "Don't be silly, bro. I'm way too heavy. Besides, I'm a stretcher case. Drive back to Gibson Station and get them to call the Flying Doctor."

We had passed the Gibson Station homestead on the way to the cave. It was four hours to the north.

"I've never driven that far," I said doubtfully.

"If you can drive two miles," Nathan said, "you can drive two hundred."

It was Nathan who'd taught me how to drive, on an abandoned mining site near our home town, Crocodile Bridge. But driving around a disused quarry was different from finding my way through two hundred miles of sandy desert.

"What if I get lost?"

"You won't get lost, Sam. Head straight for Camel's Hump. Just before you reach it, you'll come across a track. Turn left, and it'll take you all the way to Gibson Station."

He made it sound easy. But Nathan was an adult, he'd been driving for years, plus he knew the Top End like the back of his hand. I was only fourteen. Too young to have a license. And this was my first time in the desert.

"You can do it," Nathan said, sensing the doubts running through my mind. He gave me another wobbly smile. "My life is in your hands, little brother."

I tried to smile back, but failed. He wasn't joking. His life *was* in my hands. Nobody knew where we were, not even our parents. They had taken the twins to Darwin for a few days and let me stay at Nathan's. They didn't know about our trip to the desert. The trip I had pestered Nathan into making. It was my fault that this had happened. Everything was my fault. And if I didn't get help, my brother was going to end up as dead as the prehistoric kangaroo we'd just found.

"I'll be as quick as I can," I said.

The car keys were in Nathan's pocket. I had to get them out myself, because his right arm was broken. He wanted me to take his mobile phone and GPS, but they were both in his backpack, which was buried somewhere underneath him – there was no way I could get to it. I hadn't brought a backpack, but there were two granola bars and half a bar of chocolate in my pockets. I left them with Nathan, along with the water bottle I'd had clipped to my belt. Nathan's flashlight had been smashed by the cave-in. I couldn't give him mine because I needed it to find my way out. It was horrible leaving him there, all alone and badly injured in the pitch-black cave. Last thing before I left, I removed my jacket and tucked it around him.

"I'll be back before you know it."

"You take it easy," Nathan called after me. "Don't drive more than forty miles per hour. It won't help either of us if you don't get to Gibson Station in one piece."

"Sure," I said, careful not to look back. There were tears in my eyes that I didn't want Nathan to see. "Catch you later."

"Later," my brother said, just a croaky voice in the darkness behind me. I scrambled over the first rock fall and began the long, dangerous climb back to the desert's surface.

COMING THROUGH!

I stopped and listened. What was that noise? It came from somewhere up ahead. It sounded like leaves rustling. But there were no trees or bushes directly outside the cave mouth. Just spinifex, a rocky outcrop, then nothing but red scrubby desert for hundreds of miles in every direction. I held my breath and concentrated on the sound. Was it a sandstorm? It didn't sound like sand – it was too rustley, too *slithery*. My skin prickled.

Could it be something alive?

A snake, for example.

I shone the flashlight up the steep, rocky tunnel ahead of me. Nothing was there, just a few spiders' webs and shadows. Whatever was making the rustley, slithery noise was further ahead. Closer to the cave mouth. *Outside* the cave mouth, I hoped. It was probably just the wind.

What wind? I asked myself. It had been totally calm when Nathan and I entered the cave. But that had been nearly an hour ago. The weather could have changed since then.

Thoughts of Nathan focused my mind. I was supposed to be going for help. My badly injured brother was depending on me. This wasn't the time to get spooked by strange noises. I started forward again.

The noise slowly grew louder. And scarier.

Rustle, rustle, slither, slither.

If it was coming from outside the cave mouth, why couldn't I see a glow of daylight ahead?

Moments later, I did see a glow. But it wasn't daylight. I came around a slight bend and there, about forty yards further up the tunnel, was a narrow strip of starlight. *Stars!* I'd forgotten it was already late afternoon by the time Nathan and I had reached the cave. Night must have fallen while we'd been underground.

Would I be able to find my way to Gibson Station in the dark?

No longer thinking about the rustling sound, I labored up the sloping tunnel towards the cave mouth. But I didn't get far. After only two or three paces, I stopped in my tracks.

Something was there. Halfway between me and the strip of starry sky. Something with eyes.

From the size of them, I guessed the eyes belonged to a small creature – a mouse or a lizard. Nothing to worry about. I began creeping forward again, my flashlight trained on the eyes. All around them, the cave floor was strewn with small stones. And here's something weird – the stones seemed to be *moving*.

How ridiculous! I thought. *As if stones could move.* It was just shadows cast by the wavering flashlight beam. I kept going. But the nearer I got to them, the more the stones seemed to twitch and weave. Even when I held the flashlight still. The rustling noise was growing steadily louder too. When I was seven or eight yards from the eyes, my foot crunched on something that squirmed under my boot. I hopped backwards and shone the flashlight down.

Shishkebab!

My feet went on autopilot, backpedaling away from the freakish sight lit up by the flashlight beam.

What had looked like stones from a distance were actually huge brown scorpions! Hundreds of them. Ahead of me, the cave floor was a living, moving, carpet of the horrible things.

I retreated halfway back to the bend in the tunnel. My heart was still thudding like a bongo drum as I moved the flashlight beam over the horde of scorpions blocking my escape. Except for a few of the nearer ones, which were watching me with shining eyes and their stingers raised, the army of oversized arachnids was scuttling steadily away from me – up towards the star-filled cave mouth. As they moved forward, more scorpions wriggled out through a narrow fissure in the cave wall and joined the rear of the rustling, bustling swarm.

I have no idea how many there were. Hundreds, perhaps thousands. They must have lived in a secret den behind the wall. Because the cave was so isolated, and the habitat around the cave was probably ideal for the tiny creatures that scorpions feed on, the colony had bred to plague proportions.

Scorpions are nocturnal, I suddenly remembered. That's why Nathan and I hadn't seen any on the way in. But now it was nighttime. The scorpions had woken up and were on their way out for a night's hunting.

I'd be okay, I realized, as long as I waited until the last of them had disappeared out into the desert beyond the cave entrance.

But how long would that take? I shone the flashlight on the crack in the cave wall. A procession of scorpions came streaming out. The flow seemed endless.

I had a sudden brainwave. The fissure was only about an inch wide. Maybe I could block it, trapping the rest of the scorpions in their lair. Then it would take only a few minutes for the cave ahead of me to clear. I collected a handful of rocks and began tossing them into the fissure. But as fast as I tossed them in, the huge scorpions pushed them back out. They were like miniature bulldozers. Or tanks. Enraged by the assault, several of the horrible creatures went into attack mode. They came scuttling towards me with their pincers spread and their stingers curled forward over their backs like deadly hypodermic needles. I quickly backed away.

It was no good. I was trapped. I retreated another ten yards and sat down to wait until the coast was clear.

But could I really afford to wait? Somewhere in the inky depths of the cave behind me, Nathan lay badly injured. He reckoned he had cracked ribs. What if he had other internal injuries? He might even be dying as I sat there. There was no time to lose. I had to go for help.

And I had to go now.

A scorpion sting won't kill you, I told myself, as I pulled my socks up over the cuffs of my jeans. But these were *big* scorpions. And there were hundreds of them. If I fell over ...

"I'm *not* going to fall over!" I said aloud, tying my boot laces in two firm double knots.

I was wearing a pair of Nathan's jungle boots. They were half a size too big for me, but my brother wouldn't let me go into the cave in my sneakers.

"Number one rule in adventuring," he'd said, tossing the boots to me as we got out of the Land Cruiser. "Take care of your feet."

At the time I'd thought he was being too fussy,

but now I was grateful to be wearing Nathan's tall leather boots. Already they had saved me from being stung when I'd accidentally trodden on a scorpion. Could they save me again? Several hundred times?

I stood up. Thirty yards up the tunnel was the slit of starlight that marked the mouth of the cave. Focusing on the stars, I took several deep breaths, wiped my sweaty palms on my jeans and nervously wet my lips. Then I began a slow countdown. *Five, four, three, two, one.*

"Coming through!" I yelled.

5

HEADLIGHTS

It didn't seem like thirty yards – it seemed like two hundred. I ran in slow motion, like someone in a nightmare with nightmare creatures snapping at their heels. But this wasn't a bad dream, and the creatures weren't imaginary. They were real. And they were deadly.

I'm dead! I thought, with every crunching, sliding, heart-stopping step.

Despite what I'd told myself earlier, I knew the risk I was taking. I'm allergic to bee venom, which means I'm probably allergic to scorpion venom as well. And scorpions have much more venom than bees. All it would take was a single one to get flicked up onto my calf and sting me through my jeans, and I'd be cactus. And so would Nathan, because his life depended on my survival.

"Yaaaaaaaaaah!" I yelled across the last ten yards. My voice echoed through the cave and mostly drowned out the horrible crunching of my boots across the squirming carpet of arachnids.

When I burst out of the cave, the illusion of being in a dream suddenly deserted me. It was replaced by a heart-in-the-mouth sensation of zero gravity.

I was falling.

In my panic to get across the army of scorpions, I'd forgotten where the cave mouth was situated: on the side of a small, rocky escarpment, nine feet above the surrounding desert.

I landed in a thicket of spinifex. That's what saved me. Nine feet is a long way to fall and land flat on your back, but the spinifex cushioned my landing. No bones were broken. I wasn't even winded. But landing on spinifex is like landing in a cactus garden. Several thousand tiny needles jabbed through my clothing. Luckily I was wearing my bike helmet – it protected my head and the top of my neck – but the rest of me, fifty percent of my body, legs, arms, even the backs of my hands, felt like it had just received a giant tattoo.

For a few seconds I lay there in shock, spread-eagle, staring up at the wide, starry sky through a pool of gathering tears. Then I screamed.

Sound travels a long way in the desert at night. If there was anyone within five miles, they probably would have heard me. But I was all alone. There was only Nathan, deep underground, and I didn't think my scream would have carried all the way down the long, winding tunnel to where he lay. At least, I hoped not. He wouldn't have known what was going on. He might have thought I had just died.

I *felt* like I'd died. The pain was that bad. Clenching my teeth, I rolled slowly out of the spinifex. With every movement, a hundred new prickles spiked me through my clothes. It was agony. By the time I was clear of the thicket, there was hardly an inch of skin on my body that hadn't received the pins and needles treatment. Only my head and feet had been spared, thanks to my helmet and the boots I had on – and thanks to Nathan, for insisting I wear them before we went underground. My jeans had helped a little too – especially where there were seams or double layers of denim, like zippers and pockets – and again it was Nathan who'd made me change out of my shorts. I owed him a lot.

But for a while, I forgot all about him. I was in too much pain. Twisting and squirming like a demented belly dancer in the desert starlight, I could think only about removing prickles. It was nearly impossible. I'd lost my flashlight in the spinifex and couldn't see what I was doing. I shuffled over to the Land Cruiser and opened the door. The interior light didn't work (good one, Nathan!) so I had to turn on the headlights.

Even being able to see didn't help much. Standing in front of the vehicle, I discovered that most of the prickles had broken off beneath the skin. The best I could do was rub them. It seemed to help. After a few minutes, the pain began to subside into an all-over itch. I stopped scratching long enough to unhook one of the water bags hanging from the Land Cruiser's bull bar. My mouth was dry.

But I didn't get to drink. I didn't even get the cap off the big, damp water bag. Because I saw something on the horizon that made me forget about my thirst.

Headlights!

Hitching the water bag back where it came from, I jumped into the Land Cruiser, started it up and swung it around in a wide, bumpy U-turn. *Don't drive more than forty miles per hour*, Nathan had told me. But this was an emergency. The other vehicle was so far away that its headlights appeared as one single bright light on the horizon. It wasn't coming directly towards me, but seemed to be moving slowly from right to left. I had to catch up with it before it went past. I steered a course slightly ahead of the distant vehicle and, dismissing Nathan's advice, planted my foot.

Big mistake. You can't drive at full speed in the desert at night, especially if you're not on a road or a track. There are bushes, straggly trees, dry creek beds.

And animals.

The kangaroos came out of nowhere. Suddenly they were directly ahead, a group of tall, ghostly shapes that went gliding in front of the Land Cruiser. I don't know how many there were. Six or seven. I slammed on the brakes, but the big four-wheel drive was traveling too fast. It went into a long, shuddering skid. The leading animals managed to leap out of the way, but there were two more bounding along behind. We were on a collision course. One kangaroo jumped high in the air. It flew right over the Land Cruiser without even touching the roof rack. The last one wasn't so lucky. Blinded by the headlights, it swerved the wrong way. I couldn't do anything. It was too late to turn. The brake pedal was pressed right to the floor. I closed my eyes and hoped for the best.

There was a sickening thud.

6

CAR CHASE

At first I was more annoyed than upset. Why had the kangaroo jumped across the path of the Land Cruiser? It must have seen my headlights and heard me coming. Now I had to stop. With every wasted second, the vehicle crossing the horizon was getting further away. If I didn't catch up, I would have to drive all the way to Gibson Station to get help.

But I couldn't drive on without first checking the kangaroo. It might just be injured, rather than dead. I had run into the poor creature, now it was my responsibility to help it.

The kangaroo wasn't moving. I dragged it out from under the bull bar. Crouching in the Land

Cruiser's bright headlights, I checked the lifeless body for a pulse. Nothing. I felt a bit sick. And guilty. The kangaroo had died because of me. I had ignored Nathan's advice and driven too fast.

The other headlights were still there, moving slowly along the horizon. They didn't seem any closer than before. But they didn't seem further away, either. Weird.

I hopped back into the Land Cruiser and backed up four or five yards so I could drive around the carcass. But a tiny movement in its red-brown flank made me pause. Leaning forward against the steering wheel, I strained my eyes through the dusty windshield. There it was again: a slight twitch in the kangaroo's side. My skin prickled. I'd checked for a heartbeat and felt nothing. But I wasn't a vet; I could have been mistaken. I put the hand brake on and got out. As I walked slowly towards the carcass, I saw another twitch. My heart skipped a beat. The kangaroo was alive!

I was right *and* wrong. Something *was* alive, but not the kangaroo I'd hit. Seconds later, the mystery resolved itself. From out of the dead animal's fur, two tiny ears appeared, followed by a pair of wet black eyes. Then a tiny, triangular head popped up.

A joey!

I gently lifted the baby kangaroo from its mother's pouch. "Hey, Joey," I whispered, as it softly nuzzled my thumb. "I'm sorry about your mum."

It was the size of a rat, with a pencil-thin tail and long, ridiculously gangly back legs. From the way it sucked at my fingers, I realized the miniature 'roo still needed its mother's milk. But she was dead – I'd killed her. So it was up to me to take her place.

Nathan had packed some condensed milk with our supplies, but there wasn't time to dig it out. Joey would have to wait until I caught up with the vehicle on the horizon. My brother was still my number one priority. I tucked in my shirt, then undid the three top buttons and slid Joey inside, hoping it would make a passable pouch. Then I jumped back into the Land Cruiser and set off in pursuit of the distant headlights.

This time I drove slower. I'd learned my lesson. Joey was an orphan because of my reckless driving. Now his survival depended on me. As did Nathan's. I wasn't going to take any more risks.

I followed the headlights for another fifteen or twenty minutes, but I didn't seem to be getting any closer. It was weird. The other vehicle was moving away from me, yet I could see its headlights, not its tail lights. Was it *backing up*? Whenever I came to the top of a small rise, I flashed my own headlights and beeped the horn, but I couldn't attract the other driver's attention. He was too far away. He was *always* too far away. What was going on?

Finally I'd had enough. I couldn't spend the whole night involved in a bizarre car chase with a crazy driver who was speeding through the desert in reverse. The way things were going, I might run out of gas before I caught up with him. I couldn't take that risk. Nathan's life depended on me getting help. I stopped the Land Cruiser at the top of a small sand dune and got out.

"Heeeey!" I yelled, in a last-ditch effort to attract the other driver's attention. My shouting caused Joey to change position inside my shirt, but made no difference to the lights. They kept moving slowly away from me across the dark desert landscape.

Now that I was on higher ground, I noticed something strange. The other car was no longer on the horizon. In fact, it seemed quite close. Being careful not to squash Joey, I clambered up onto the

Land Cruiser's roof rack for a better view. What I saw gave me quite a shock.

It wasn't headlights. It was just a single ball of bluish-white light. Totally confused, I watched it moving up a sand dune no more than three hundred yards away. When it reached the top, it rose clear of the dunes and hung suspended in the sky. It seemed to wobble for a moment, then it slowly faded away, until nothing was left but stars.

I started shivering, even though it wasn't cold. Now I knew what I'd been following for the past half hour.

The Min Min light.

7

TOTALLY LOST

Lots of people have seen the Min Min light, but nobody can explain what it is. Some scientists think it's a kind of mirage caused by thermal layers in the air that bend light sources from a long way away and make them appear somewhere else. Other people reckon it's fireflies. Or flying saucers. There are even those who say it's a ghost.

I don't know what to believe. All I know is this: *I saw it.* For half an hour I followed the Min Min light through the desert. It led me on a wild goose chase, then disappeared into thin air.

I stood on the Land Cruiser's roof and turned in a slow circle. Where was Camel's Hump? When Nathan gave me directions to Gibson Station, he was in shock from the accident and hadn't remembered that it would be dark by the time I found my way out from underground. I had no idea where I was. No idea which way I'd driven when I left the cave, nor how far I'd come. And Nathan was back there (wherever "there" was), a third of a mile below ground. Waiting for me to get help.

Now *I* needed help. I lifted Joey out of my shirt. "We're lost," I whispered.

A meteor fell through the sky, trailing a long line of sparks all the way to the horizon. I made a silent wish. But I was fourteen, too old for wishes. And too young to be stuck in the middle of a desert with the responsibility of my brother's life on my shoulders.

A small section of the horizon was clearly visible where the meteor had disappeared. It was where the sun must have set, leaving a faint trace of daylight in the sky. Suddenly something occurred to me. The sun sets in the west. I turned ninety degrees to my right. Now I was facing north.

I had gotten my wish.

"Joey," I said, carefully replacing the little kangaroo inside my shirt, "we're in business."

I drove in first gear. Every two or three minutes, I

would stop and switch the headlights off, to check that the pale section of sky was still to my left. After stopping a few times, I noticed something weird. Instead of growing darker as the sun moved further around the other side of the earth, the pale patch of sky was becoming steadily brighter. I couldn't figure it out.

Then the rim of a large yellow disk slowly nudged up over the horizon.

I jammed on the brakes. *Sam Fox, you're an idiot!* I thought. For twenty minutes I'd been navigating by the light of the rising moon.

Where did the moon rise? Did it rise in the east like the sun? I wondered. *Or in the west? Or in the south?* I had no idea. Now I was *totally* lost. I switched off the engine and sat back in my seat.

"Face it, Fox," I muttered aloud. "You've messed up big time."

It was partly Nathan's fault, I decided. (I was looking for someone else to blame.) He was a tour guide; he should have had a two-way radio in his Land Cruiser. Or a compass, at the very least. But this wasn't his work vehicle. All he'd brought along was his cell phone and his GPS. Both were in his backpack, buried underneath him at the bottom of the cave.

He'd brought a map too, I suddenly remembered. It was on the dashboard. I unfolded it on the seat beside me, then rummaged in the glove compartment for the cigarette lighter Nathan kept there for lighting campfires. I used its flickering flame to study the map.

Nathan had marked the cave and its GPS coordinates in blue pen. Camel's Hump was about half an inch to the northeast, and Gibson Station homestead was another eight inches above that. Apart from those two landmarks, it was mostly empty desert in all directions. Particularly to the south, where the desert ran right off the edge of the map. I hoped with all my heart that I hadn't driven south.

As I refolded the map and stuck it in my pocket, Joey began wriggling inside my shirt. He started about fifty spinifex tips itching beneath my skin. I lifted him out and had a scratch. When the worst of the itching had subsided, I became aware of another discomfort – *inside* my stomach, not outside. I was hungry.

"I think it's dinnertime, Joey," I said.

Nathan reckons there's nothing better than big, hearty meals when you're out in the bush. We'd planned to camp overnight at the cave, but my brother had packed enough food to last a week! I felt a bit guilty biting into an enormous salami, cheese and baked bean sandwich when he only had two granola bars and some chocolate, but I figured I should keep my strength up – who knew what tomorrow would bring.

Joey was hungry too. After my third sandwich, I opened a can of condensed milk and fed him by dipping my finger in and letting him lick it off. The little kangaroo seemed to like the thick, sweet liquid and polished off nearly half the can before he snuggled up inside my shirt and fell asleep. I finished off the rest of the condensed milk with some canned peaches for dessert, then washed everything down with some orange juice straight from the bottle. Afterwards, I packed all the food away and dragged out my sleeping bag.

I had decided to stay where I was overnight, rather than drive on blindly and risk getting even more lost. But as I unrolled my sleeping bag on the Land Cruiser's back seat, I heard something that changed my plans.

Thumpa thumpa thumpa thumpa.

I knew that noise. Twice in the past, it had spelled the difference between my living or dying. With my heart belting like a punching bag inside my rib cage, I searched the night sky. There it was! A tiny, blinking light, paler than the surrounding stars, moved swiftly across the sky. Even though it was several thousand feet above me, the sound of the helicopter's rotor was loud in the huge, empty desert. I jumped into the front seat and began madly blinking the Land Cruiser's headlights. Three short flashes, three long flashes, then three short: Morse code for SOS.

The helicopter changed course. For a few moments I thought the pilot had seen me. But instead of circling back in my direction, the blinking light descended at a sharp angle, dropping straight down into the desert. It sank from view below the distant sand dunes, and the thump of its rotor faded into silence.

It had landed!

I clambered back up onto the roof rack. I couldn't see the helicopter, but I knew it was in the desert just over the horizon. Three or four miles away, I estimated. Six, maximum. Even driving in first gear, I could be there in half an hour.

Swinging down into the driver's seat, I set the Land Cruiser on a course directly towards the three bright stars that pointed in a line to the place where the helicopter had disappeared. As long as it didn't take off again in the next thirty minutes, Nathan would be rescued within a matter of hours.

8

HORROR MOVIE

Flump, flump, flump, flump went the flat tire.

Twice before I'd been in a vehicle when a tire went flat, but on those occasions I hadn't been driving. The Land Cruiser felt like it was drunk. It swayed and lurched. The steering wheel dragged hard to the left, then pulled wickedly to the right. I couldn't drive in a straight line. The engine roared. The doors rattled. Tools and cooking equipment crashed around in the back. Finally, halfway down a sand dune, the vehicle slewed sharply sideways and nearly rolled.

This is madness! I thought, switching off the engine. When I'd first gotten the flat I'd kept driving because I knew how difficult it would be to change a wheel in the dark. And how much time it would take. All I could think about was reaching the helicopter before it took off again. But five minutes of driving on a flat tire had nearly ended in disaster. I would have to change it.

Which was fine in theory. Problem was, I had never changed a tire in my life. And the Land Cruiser was halfway down a steep slope, tilted dangerously to one side and buried nearly up to its axles in sand. I had to get it onto level ground before I could safely use the jack. That meant driving down to the bottom of the sand dune. When I got back in and started the engine, the Land Cruiser wouldn't move. It was stuck.

Plan B. I would have to walk.

Here's another of Nathan's survival rules: *When you get lost or stranded in the outback, stay with your vehicle until help arrives. But how long would that take?* I wondered. Nobody knew we were missing. And they wouldn't know until Nathan failed to show up for work on Monday morning. Today was Saturday. There was enough food and drink in the Land Cruiser to keep me going for a fortnight. But Nathan only had two granola bars, some chocolate and half a bottle of water. Plus he was badly injured. I had no choice but to leave my vehicle and go for help.

I didn't know how far I had come since I'd seen the helicopter. Two or three miles, I guessed. The helicopter couldn't be too far away. I took Joey with me. And one of the water bags, just in case. But I was pretty confident I could find my way. All I had to do was walk towards the three bright stars.

After twenty minutes, I began to feel less sure about things. The three stars seemed to be higher in the night sky, and the line they made was no longer perpendicular. It tipped slightly to the right. I figured out what was going on. The movement of the earth had changed the position of the stars in relation to the horizon. Major bummer! It meant they would no longer lead me to the helicopter.

Uncertain what to do, I put the waterbag down and cupped both hands around my mouth. "Cooee!" I called, as loud as I could, hoping the pilot would hear. I don't know if he heard, but something did. It answered with a high, mournful howl that made my hair stand up and caused Joey to shift nervously inside my shirt.

A dingo.

Moments later, the wild dog howled again. Or was that another one? The second howl sounded closer.

Dingoes aren't dangerous, I told myself, as I strained my eyes in the direction of the eerie, blood-chilling sound. There had been hardly any cases of them attacking people. It was only semi-wild dingoes that were a threat. Animals that lived near popular tourist destinations, who had lost their natural caution around humans. I was in the middle of a desert, hundreds of miles from the nearest tourist attraction. I had nothing to fear.

Or so I thought.

The dingo howled again. It was difficult to judge how close it was, or in what direction. The sound seemed to come from all around me, like in a movie theater with multiple speakers. It rang through the wide, starry sky and sent a shiver to every part of my body. If I were at the movies, this would be a horror film. Joey had stopped fidgeting, but I could feel his tiny, racing heartbeat against my itchy stomach.

"It's okay, Joey," I whispered, stroking him through my shirt. I wanted to call out to the helicopter pilot again, but I was too scared to raise my voice. I didn't want the dingo – or dingoes – to know where I was.

Too late. Out of the corner of my eye, I glimpsed a movement at the top of a nearby sand dune. Or had I imagined it? By the time I turned my head, nothing was there. The dune made a long, smooth silhouette against a thousand twinkling stars. The moon was still low in the sky, casting the near face of the dune in deep shadow. I strained my eyes. It was all shadows, black on black. Slowly I backed away, out of the dune's shadow and into the pale moonlight.

I stopped. Something was behind me. I could hear its breath, a rapid, in-out rush of air, like a dog panting. Very slowly, taking care not to make any sudden movements, I turned around. Nothing. Just an empty expanse of moonlit sand. *Just my imagination*, I told myself. I felt weak with relief.

Then I saw a trail of shadow-filled indentations in the sand. Animal footprints. It didn't take a genius to figure out what kind of animal. The dingo had been stalking me from behind. It had come as close as ten yards, then melted back into the shadows when I'd turned around.

I backed away from the footprints in a cold

sweat, as if they were alive. After two or three paces, I made myself stop. Panicking wasn't going to help. The dingo was out there in the darkness. It knew where I was. It was probably watching me at that very moment. *But it's afraid of me*, I said to myself. Otherwise, why had it run away when I'd turned around?

Encouraged by this thought, I forced myself to calm down. I had to think rationally. I had to figure out what to do. The dingo was out there, but it was scared of me, so it wasn't my biggest problem. Getting help for Nathan was still my top concern. I had to find the helicopter.

I clambered to the crest of a sand dune and cupped my hands around my mouth. "Cooee!" I yelled.

In the distance, a dingo howled. Another one answered from no more than fifty yards away. Then a third dingo howled somewhere behind me. How many dingoes were there?

"*Coooooeeeeee!*" I screamed.

About five dingoes answered, but no humans. I tried again and again, until my throat was sore, and I had run out of breath. No one responded. By now, the line of three bright stars had moved so far from the horizon that I didn't even know in which direction to shout.

I had to face facts: I wasn't going to find the helicopter in the dark. I would have to wait until daylight. That meant spending the night in the desert.

Nathan was right. I should never have left the Land Cruiser. But it was too late now. I looked around for somewhere to sleep. Not that I really expected to get any sleep. The dingoes had stopped howling, but I was worried about them. Especially the one that had stalked me. Now that they were silent, I had no idea where they were. I stroked Joey's tiny head with one finger. Small as he was, at least he was company.

I decided to stay where I was. I would spend the night at the top of the sand dune. From there, I had a good view of the desert around me. The moon made the scene surprisingly bright. I could even see my own footprints, crossing another sand dune seventy or eighty yards away.

That's it! said a little voice in my head. I could follow my footprints. They would lead me back to the Land Cruiser.

I was so relieved about not having to spend the

night out in the open, I completely forgot about
the dingoes until I reached the bottom of the dune.
Then I heard a tiny noise. Or thought I did. I glanced
nervously over my shoulder.

Shishkebab!

Silhouetted against the night sky, a line of ghostly,
wolf-like forms came slinking down the slope behind
me.

HUMAN PREY

Don't run, I told myself.

Dingoes are social animals. On their own they are naturally timid, but put them with others of their kind and a pack mentality takes over. They draw courage from each other. They become bold. And there's nothing that makes a dingo pack bolder, and therefore more dangerous, than something (or someone) running away from it.

Even knowing that, it's hard not to run when there are half a dozen ravenous dingoes creeping along behind you in the dark.

I knew they were ravenous because I could see the bumps of their ribs in the moonlight. These dingoes were all skin and bone. They were half-starved; their hunger overrode their natural caution. To them, I had ceased being a human. I was prey.

To make matters worse, I had Joey tucked down in my shirt. I must have smelled of kangaroo – and baby kangaroo, at that. To a dingo, a baby kangaroo is the greatest delicacy on the face of the earth.

I have to admit … several times I considered tossing Joey to the dingoes. It might have gotten them off my case, distracted them long enough to allow me to make a run for it. But I couldn't do it. I had already killed Joey's mother; I couldn't kill him too.

Besides, I wasn't sure that sacrificing Joey would save my life anyway. It might do just the opposite. Once the starving dingoes got a taste of blood, they might lose the last scrap of natural caution that had stopped them from attacking me so far. Joey would be the appetizer – I would be the main course.

The dingoes were still a tiny bit scared of me. They hung back. But when I tried walking faster, they increased their pace. When I slowed down, my silent pursuers slowed too. Each time I looked over my shoulder, the six stalking shadows were still there. And always slightly closer. At first they stayed about fifteen yards back, then the distance was down to ten. Now it was only five or six.

I had to do something. There were no trees to climb, and I was only about halfway back to the Land Cruiser. Still five or six minutes from safety. I sensed that the dingoes weren't going to wait that long. At any moment, one of them might build up the courage to lead the others across the five-yard gap separating us. And I knew which one that would be.

Every pack has its leader, its alpha dog. The leader in this case was unmistakable. Its fur was pitch-black, and it stood a head taller than the other animals. Because it was black, it was nearly invisible, except in direct moonlight. It wasn't a pure dingo; it looked like a cross between a dingo and a Doberman. Being a cross made it more dangerous than the others. It had less natural fear of humans. It was the alpha dog, always at the front of the pack. The one that would lead the attack.

Unless I attacked first.

I swung around and faced them.

The pack stopped. The five smaller animals edged slowly away from me, until they were behind the tall black dingo/Doberman cross. We squared up to each other in the moonlight. There were only three yards between us. My heart was beating like a jackhammer. The alpha dog let out a long, low growl. Its eyes glinted in the moonlight. An ear flicked. Otherwise it didn't move. It was waiting to see what I would do next.

There was a large, circular spinifex bush about three feet to my right. Not taking my eyes off the big black mongrel, I shuffled slowly sideways and bent over. About fifty needle-sharp prickles jabbed through my skin, but I hardly noticed the pain as I ripped up a large handful of dry, straw-like spinifex. I slid my other hand into my pocket.

This had better work, I thought.

I thumbed the flint of Nathan's cigarette lighter. It made a loud, rasping click, and sparks flew. That was all – there was no flame. My hand was shaking; my fingers felt damp with sweat. I clicked the lighter a second time. Same result. The alpha dog growled again and lowered its head. It was getting ready to spring. I clicked the lighter again. Success! A tiny blue-and-yellow flame shot up. It reflected in the alpha dog's eyes and glinted on its long, bared teeth. The animal was crouched low to the ground, growling deep in its throat. At any moment, it was going to launch itself at me.

Don't make any sudden moves, I cautioned myself. Slowly, I lifted the flaming cigarette lighter towards the bunch of spinifex in my other hand. But even as the first spiky tips began to ignite, I realized it was too late.

The alpha dog sprang.

Whumph! The spinifex exploded into a bright, crackling fireball.

For a moment it blinded me. But it blinded my attacker too. Unable to see, the flying dog smashed into my chest paws first, rather than jaws first. It bowled me over backwards. We landed in a tangle of legs and arms. The mongrel was on top of me, but I had surprise on my side. Before it had time to recover, I waved the fiercely burning spinifex in its face. It twisted away with a yelp of fright. I rolled over and went after it, scrambling along on my knees, waving my flaming torch in front of me and yelling for all I was worth. The alpha dog didn't know what was happening, only that it was being attacked by something hot and bright and loud. It went bounding off into the darkness, whimpering like an overgrown puppy. The rest of the pack milled around me for a few frightening moments, then they scattered and went chasing after their leader.

All but one. The remaining animal was six or seven yards away, nose to the sand as it followed a fresh scent along the ground.

"Yaaaah!" I yelled, scrambling to my feet and waving my fiery torch.

The dingo raised its head slightly, but not to look at me. The focus of its attention was a small clump of spinifex. From where I stood, I could see something on the opposite side of the bush – a tiny, quivering form that cowered as the larger animal approached.

With a gasp of shock, I realized what it was. A baby kangaroo.

10

IF FOURTEEN-YEAR-OLDS HAD HEART ATTACKS

Sometime during my battle with the alpha dog, my shirt had come untucked, allowing Joey to fall out. Now the baby kangaroo huddled helplessly behind the spinifex clump as the dingo crept towards it. I was sideways to the drama; I could see exactly what was about to happen.

I yelled again, but the dingo paid no attention. It probably hadn't eaten for a week, and it was hot on the scent of every dingo's favorite meal. My flaming torch had burned down to my hand, forcing me to drop it. There wasn't time to make another one, and anyway, I had lost Nathan's lighter. I raced across the moonlit sand, waving both arms and yelling like a madman. I had no plan. I didn't know what I was going to do if the dingo didn't run away, but I couldn't let it eat Joey. It paused just long enough to flash its teeth in my direction, then turned and pounced across the spinifex.

"Nooooooo!" I cried, hurling myself headlong through the air.

I caught the dingo in a flying tackle, knocking it to one side. I landed on top. Because the animal was so skinny, I nearly crushed it. There was a whoosh of air being driven from its lungs and the horrible sound of a rib cracking. It let out a yowl of pain and bit me on the shoulder.

Luckily it was only a glancing bite – more a nip, really – and I managed to roll away before the dingo could bite me again. But I rolled into a wall of spinifex.

It wasn't the clump that Joey had hidden behind. This was a much larger one. It prickled me in about a hundred different places through my shirt, but still I pressed backwards into it. I was cornered.

The dingo came stalking towards me, crouched low to the ground, limping slightly. It had forgotten about the baby kangaroo now – all its hate and anger was focused on me. I had attacked it, so the dingo probably saw me as a threat to its life. It was coming to finish me off.

There wasn't time to stand up. I grabbed two handfuls of spinifex, ripping them out by their roots. As the dingo rushed forward, I thrust them in front of me. The unfortunate animal ran straight into them with its mouth wide-open.

It must have been like biting a cactus. The dingo let out an ear-splitting howl, then turned and went limping off into the night, shaking its head and stopping every few paces to rub its nose with its paws. I felt sorry for it later, but at the time I was just grateful to be alive.

I was shaking like a leaf as I made my way over to the smaller clump of spinifex. The baby kangaroo huddled in the shadows. He was shaking too.

"It's okay, Joey," I said, giving him a gentle cuddle, then placing him carefully back inside my shirt. "You're safe n– "

I didn't finish the sentence. I might have saved my breath anyway, because Joey wasn't safe. Neither was I. But I didn't realize it right away. I was too amazed by what I saw.

What on earth … ?

First I'd seen the Min Min light, now there was another weird light. On the front of my shirt. Exactly where Joey was. It was pink and round, about the size of a bottle cap, and it was moving. As I watched dumbfounded, it came wobbling slowly up my shirt front, then stopped on my chest, slightly to the left of center. Right on my heart.

I looked at it for a moment, then the truth hit me like a hammer.

Holy guacamole!

If fourteen-year-olds had heart attacks, I probably would have dropped dead right there and then. Instead, my heart went into hyperdrive, my body switched over to autopilot and adrenaline kicked in. I hurled myself sideways.

And not a second too soon. As the little pink light went skidding off the edge of my khaki shirt, the deafening *crack-crack-crack* of automatic gunfire shattered the silence of the desert night.

11

TRAPPED

I lay inside a circle of spinifex, peering out through a tiny gap as four shadowy figures with guns cast around on the sand for my footprints. One of them had a flashlight. He cupped his hand around its lens, making a narrow beam that swept to and fro across the red, bumpy ground. This was where I'd fought the dingoes, and there were footprints and dog tracks leading everywhere.

"I'm sure I got him," one of the armed men whispered angrily. "He should have gone down."

I bit my lower lip to stop my teeth from chattering; I didn't want to give my position away. My insides had turned to jelly. With one hand, I nervously stroked Joey. Who were these men? They were dressed like soldiers and carried automatic weapons with state-of-the-art, infrared night sights. It didn't make sense. There wasn't a war on.

Then it hit me. Terrorists! I had nearly blundered into a terrorist training camp. That explained the helicopter landing in the middle of the desert under the cover of darkness. It explained the uniforms, the weapons, and why the four men were after me. I was a threat to their secret operation. They wanted me dead.

"Over here!" hissed the man with the flashlight. "He went this way."

They had found the tracks I'd made when I'd left the Land Cruiser. Luckily the sand was soft, and they couldn't see that the footprints were actually coming towards them, not going away.

"Follow me," the man said.

As the four terrorists went creeping off into the darkness, I jumped up and headed in the opposite direction. I ducked across a low dune and started running. I wanted to put as much distance as possible between me and the terrorists. In five minutes they would reach the Land Cruiser and realize they had gone the wrong way. In another five minutes they would be back, going the right way this time.

I had a ten-minute head start, but that doesn't seem like much when there are men with guns coming after you. I ran blindly at first, concentrating on speed, not on where I was going. Big mistake. After a short time I had no idea which direction I was heading. It was even possible that I was running in circles. I forced myself to stop and try to figure out where I was. There were no other footprints in the moonlit sand around me. At least I wasn't back where I started. I looked up at the moon. Had it been on my left when I started running? Or on my right? I couldn't remember.

You idiot! I thought. My life hung in the balance, and I wasn't using my head.

Nathan's life hung in the balance as well. Nathan, who had been taking me out into the bush since I was about six years old and teaching me survival skills. Now, when it really mattered, I had forgotten everything he'd told me. I had let him down.

His voice back came to me now. *First rule in a tight situation: keep a cool head.*

Okay. Now I was calm. Relatively calm anyway, considering there were four armed terrorists coming after me and no help for hundreds of miles. I remembered Nathan's advice again.

Second rule: figure out your options and how likely they are to succeed.

I had two options: run away, or hide. Hiding was too risky – my tracks would lead the terrorists straight to me. So I had to keep running.

Third rule: take the most likely option, and remember to keep a cool head.

It all came back to rule one. Keep calm, use your head, think before you act. Running away from the terrorists wouldn't work if I went in circles. First I had to find out where they were, then I could use the moon as a guide to help me outrun them.

I climbed cautiously to the top of a low ridge and crouched between two clumps of spinifex. Although I kept telling myself to remain calm, my heart was galloping like the hooves of a racehorse. I scanned the moonlit desert in all directions, waiting for the terrorists to appear. It was agonizing. Where *were* they? With every passing second, I knew they were getting closer. But I couldn't run, because I didn't know which way to go. I might choose the wrong direction and run straight into them.

And then it would be *all over, red rover.*

Finally I saw a movement. First it was just the black silhouette of a man's head and shoulders rising over the crest of a nearby dune, then the winking yellow eye of a flashlight appeared. The flashlight was shining on the ground, not on me, but I froze like a possum caught in the headlights. The terrorists were only a hundred yards away, coming straight towards me. They'd see me if I moved. Cradling Joey through my shirt front, I forced myself to wait while the four stealthy figures filed down the dune into a slight dip. As soon as they were out of sight, I leapt to my feet and charged across the ridge.

For half a minute I ran flat out. Then I remembered Nathan's advice about keeping a cool head and made myself slow down. Running in sand is very tiring; I had to conserve my energy. I kept the moon on my left and tried to stay in the dips between sand dunes. When I absolutely *had* to cross ridges, I ducked down and made myself as small as possible, scooting over the skyline on all fours like a chimpanzee.

It was tough going, especially on the uphill parts, but at least I was traveling light. I only had Joey to carry, and he weighed hardly anything. My pursuers had heavy guns. It would slow them down. I tried not to think about their guns. Each time I did, a strange, prickly feeling ran up and down my spine. I kept imagining a wobbly pink dot of light on the back of my shirt. I kept expecting to hear the terrifying *crack-crack-crack* of automatic gunfire.

Instead, I heard the sound of a motorcycle.

I stopped in my tracks. The motorcycle was directly ahead, just over the next sand dune. Its headlight lit up the spinifex on the skyline. I had no illusions about it being someone coming to my rescue. It was another terrorist, for sure. I was trapped. Four terrorists on foot behind, one on a motorcycle in front. I had two choices: I could go left, or right.

I turned right. Head down, I raced along the gully between the two sand dunes. But I wasn't fast enough. With a loud roar, the motorcycle burst over the ridge only fifty yards away. It veered sharply in my direction. As its headlight came sweeping across the sand behind me, I fled like a hunted rabbit out of the end of the gully.

And ran straight into the wall of a tent.

A MATTER OF
NATIONAL SECURITY

The big, army-style tent was draped in camouflage netting to prevent it being seen from the air. The netting was like a huge, soft spider's web. It stopped Joey from being crushed by my body, but it caught me like a fly in a web. The motorcycle's bright beam swung towards me. At the very last second, I struggled free. It was too late to run. I threw myself to the ground, accidentally dragging a large section of the camouflage down on top of me.

I lay completely still, partially covered by netting. The motorcycle came roaring out of the darkness. Its headlight was trained right on me. The edges of its light revealed other camouflaged tents all around me and a helicopter forty yards away. Behind the helicopter, and also covered in netting, was a row of military vehicles, including a huge, evil-looking tank. My blood ran cold at the sight of it. Whoever these terrorists were, they were planning something big.

For a moment I considered wriggling out from under the netting and making a dash for it, but I abandoned the idea just as quickly. I had blundered right into the terrorists' secret stronghold. There was no escape. I would let them take me prisoner and try to talk my way out of it.

But I was fooling myself. The terrorists wouldn't let me go – I had seen too much. No amount of talking would save me.

The motorcycle slowed as it approached. All I could see was its headlight. It blinded me. I heard the rider change gears. There was a squeal of dusty brake pads, then the machine came to a standstill only a few yards away. The kickstand clunked down. I closed my eyes and tensed my whole body, waiting to be dragged out of my hiding place.

It didn't happen. The terrorist walked right past me, so close that I heard the swish of his boots through the sand above the soft *putter-putter* of his motorcycle in the background. He had left its engine idling. A zipper rasped, and he went into the tent.

I opened my eyes and cautiously lifted my head. I couldn't believe my good luck. The motorcyclist hadn't seen me. He had come to the tent for some other reason. I listened to him rummaging around inside. Obviously he wasn't planning on staying long because he'd left his motorcycle running and its headlight on. As soon as he rode away, I would climb out from under the netting and creep out of the terrorists' camp by the same route I'd come in.

Good plan. Except that I'd forgotten to take into account one thing. I remembered it when I saw a flash of light fifty yards away. It was a flashlight beam trained on the ground. Four shadowy figures carrying guns came creeping along the gully towards me. They were following a line of footprints that led all the way to the pile of fallen netting where I lay hiding.

There wasn't time to consider the probability of being shot. I had to act now, or I'd be captured. Heaving the camouflage netting to one side, I sprang to my feet and raced over to the idling motorcycle. There was a shout from the direction of the four terrorists and a stifled exclamation from the doorway of the tent. I paid no attention. In one fluid motion, I swung myself onto the bike, squeezed the clutch, stamped on the gearshift and gave it a fistful of throttle.

The most powerful motorcycle I'd ridden before that night was Nathan's clapped-out Yamaha 250 bush basher. This was the latest-model Kawasaki KLR650. In the power department, it would have left Nathan's heap of junk for dead.

It nearly left me for dead too.

When I poured on the juice, the rear wheel dug in, and the front wheel jerked off the ground in a massive mono. *Shishkebab!* I hung on for my life as the out-of-control Kawasaki roared between the tents on its rear wheel. I had done heaps of monos on my BMX, but this was totally different. Totally scary. I backed off the throttle, and the front wheel hit the deck with a jarring thump. Not a moment too soon. Ducking my head, I shot beneath the cannon barrel of the tank. A gun-waving terrorist wearing just an undershirt and camouflage trousers came running out of a tent. He dropped his gun and dived back into his tent as I nearly mowed him down.

A prickly sensation ran up and down my spine. I kept expecting to hear shots – I kept expecting to get shot – but all I heard above the roar of the Kawasaki's engine was a series of confused and angry shouts.

They could shout all they liked – no way was I going to stop. There was much more at stake now than my and Nathan's lives. It was a matter of national security. Someone had to warn the authorities about the terrorists.

And that person was me.

SHOOTING GALLERY

I raced past the last few tents. There was open ground ahead. My headlight lit up the tall, pale shape of a sand dune. I crouched low over the Kawasaki's gas tank, aware that I was nearly squashing Joey, but desperate to present as small a target as possible to the terrorists behind me. At any moment they would start shooting.

I rode flat out up the sand dune. The Kawasaki's engine screamed. It was still in first – I had forgotten to change gears. Actually, I was so terrified, I'd forgotten *how* to change gears. All I could focus on was getting to the top of the sand dune, getting over the top, and getting away.

But I wasn't going to get away if I continued panicking. I was only halfway up the dune, still a hundred yards from safety. I would be a sitting duck if the terrorists opened fire.

Not if *they open fire*, said a little voice in my brain. When *they open fire*.

Then I heard another voice. Nathan's. *First rule in a tight situation: keep a cool head.*

With a flick of my thumb, I switched off the Kawasaki's lights. It nearly caused a disaster. I couldn't see! I was riding blind. Desperately, I wound back the throttle, slowing the bike down. Even though I'd lost a lot of speed, I felt safer. If I couldn't see, then the terrorists couldn't see either.

I had forgotten they had infrared gun sights.

Boom!

It sounded like a cannon. My whole body tensed like a wound-up spring, waiting for the deadly impact. Nothing happened. *Missed!* I thought, and a wave of relief flooded through me.

Not for long. There was a loud *pop* high overhead, like fireworks, and suddenly night turned to day.

They had sent up a flare. It was so bright I had to screw up my eyes against the glare. I screwed the

Kawasaki's throttle grip too. And clunked the gearbox into second. I knew I was lit up like a target in a shooting gallery, and that every gun in the terrorists' camp was probably aimed at my back, but in the light of the flare I saw something that gave me the tiniest speck of hope. The crest of the dune was only ten yards away and coming up fast.

"Hold on tight," I said to Joey.

I crouched low over the handlebars and poured on the power.

The back of the sand dune fell away much more steeply than the side facing the terrorists' camp. I came over the top doing roughly fifty miles per hour and launched into space.

The Kawasaki went into free fall. Thanks to the flare, I could see the motorcycle's shadow way below me. It seemed much too small. But it was getting bigger fast – *too fast*, I thought – as the dune raced up to meet me.

Nathan had never let me do stunts on his Yamaha, but a few mates and I had built a series of BMX jumps near the garbage dump at Crocodile Bridge. I knew how to land a bike without killing myself. You have to get the front end down so that both wheels hit the

67

down slope at the same time. But a Kawasaki KLR650 is a lot different from a knee-high BMX. It's much bigger and much, *much* heavier. I only got the front halfway down before the back wheel hit.

There was a jarring impact that rattled my backbone and buckled my legs and arms. Sand exploded over me like a bomb blast. The handlebars wrenched one way, then the other, as the bike fishtailed down the steep, sandy slope. I had lost control. There was nothing I could do but hold on.

And twist the throttle.

That's what saved me. As soon as I gave it some juice, the Kawasaki straightened up. Its rear wheel found traction in the sand and away we went. Down to the bottom of the dune and up over the next one.

It wasn't until I had crossed three more low dunes and the flare had burned out, that I dared to turn the Kawasaki's lights back on. I could scarcely believe it. I had escaped!

But I knew better than to start congratulating myself. The terrorists would come after me. At the top of the next dune, I glanced over my shoulder. Sure enough, there were headlights in the distance. I hoped it wasn't the tank.

Sand is horrible to ride on. It's almost as slippery as ice. The Kawasaki slewed drunkenly from side to side. It felt like a kayak in choppy water. I was constantly using my feet to stay upright. It slowed me down. My pursuers were gaining on me. Every time I looked back, the headlights were closer.

I had no option. I switched the Kawasaki's lights back off. It was risky riding in the dark, but less risky than showing my bright red tail light, like a beacon, to the terrorists. Anyway, I wasn't riding fast – it was impossible in the deep, soft sand. My eyes soon adjusted to the moonlit landscape. It was mostly sand, with the occasional clump of spinifex or small tree. At the bottom of a dip between two dunes, I changed direction and gunned the motorcycle along the valley, hoping to throw off my pursuers. At the end of the valley, I changed direction again. I did this for several minutes, always staying in the valleys and changing direction every few hundred yards. Then I stopped the bike, switched off the engine and listened.

At first I heard nothing. My heart pumped in relief. I lifted Joey out of my shirt and softly stroked him with one fingertip between his tiny ears.

"Sorry about the rough ride," I said. "There were some bad guys after us."

It was a mistake to use past tense. The bad guys were *still* after us.

I stopped stroking Joey and carefully put him back inside my shirt. I had heard something. A faint but unmistakable hum. It was a truck or a four-wheel drive. *Or a tank*, I thought, with a sinking feeling in the pit of my stomach. I swung myself off the Kawasaki and turned in a slow circle. It was impossible to tell which direction the sound was coming from. I had to know, because I had to go in the *other* direction.

Leaving the motorcycle, I slogged up through the heavy sand to the top of a dune. Now I could hear the sound clearly. It was closer than I'd thought. I strained my eyes across the moonlit desert landscape. Was that a light I could see? A pale glow had appeared on the side of a dune three hundred yards away. As I watched, it slowly increased in brightness, until a powerful set of lights flashed into view.

It was impossible to see whether it was a truck, a four-wheel drive, or (worst-case scenario) a tank. All I could see were its lights. There were three of them. The center one, mounted higher than those on either side, was directed down at the sand just in front of the quickly moving vehicle. They were using a spotlight to follow my tire marks.

I raced back down the dune, started the Kawasaki and plowed off into the night. I didn't know what to do. The terrorists were gaining on me. And there was no way I could escape them, because the motorcycle's tracks were as obvious as arrows on a map.

It was only a matter of time before they caught up with me.

14

HUNTED ANIMAL

A huge, pale shape loomed out of the darkness ahead. I had to swerve to miss it. Another lurched across in front of me. *Kangaroos?* I wondered. But they were too big for kangaroos. I flicked the headlight on. *Holy guacamole!* I was surrounded by knobbly knees, enormous pale bodies with dusty, frayed-carpet hides and eyes that glowed green in the Kawasaki's bouncing headlight. Camels. I had ridden right into the middle of a herd of them.

They had been sleeping before I came along. Now they were staggering to their feet all around me, groaning and snorting and bumping into each other in their hurry to get out of my way. I was too surprised to hit the brakes. There wasn't time anyway. The terrorists were only a hundred yards behind, just around the last corner. I swerved to miss a camel calf and nearly had a head-on with its mother. Panicked camels were charging in all directions. A big bull swung around and roared, showering my face with a spray of evil-smelling saliva. The shaggy tail of another animal whacked me across the chest. I heaved the bike right, then left, then right again. Camels shot past me on either side. I could barely see where I was going; it was a nightmare slalom. I was riding for my life. One wrong turn, one moment's loss of control in the loose sand, and *whomp*, it would be all over – either I'd break my neck, or the terrorists would get me.

It didn't happen. Somehow I avoided the camels. Or they avoided me. Instead of running into them, I found myself riding behind a group of ten or twelve of the huge stampeding animals, like a cowboy herding cattle. I was eating their dust as they went thundering off into the night. It gave me an idea.

I switched off the headlight, waited a few seconds for my eyes to adjust, then rode right in among the herd. Two of the rear-most animals snorted in fright and peeled off to the left, but the rest continued galloping straight ahead, with me in the middle. I had the Kawasaki in third gear, and its exhaust note was pretty quiet, barely as loud as the camels' pounding hooves and their whoofing, puffing breath. In the confusion of the shadowy stampede, they must have thought I was one of them.

We continued that way for several minutes, until we came to a steep rise. Then I had to change down to first gear and pour on the juice. The Kawasaki roared. It gave the game away. Finally realizing there was an impostor in their midst, the camels scattered left and right.

But they had served their purpose. For two miles, my unwitting escorts had obliterated the Kawasaki's tire marks with their hoof prints. Back in the valley where I had disturbed the sleeping herd, the terrorists would find nothing but camel tracks leading off in all directions. They wouldn't know which trail to follow.

I had outwitted them. But only temporarily. They were terrorists; they wouldn't give up. As soon as it got light, they would find my trail again. They would come after me in their helicopter.

I rode for another hour. Several times I stopped

and checked to see if I was being followed. Except for the ticking sound of the Kawasaki's cooling engine, the desert night was silent. There were no lights in any direction. I looked up at the moon. It was behind me now. I wondered which way I was going. As long as it was away from the terrorists, I didn't care. My first priority was to avoid being caught. I would worry about finding help tomorrow.

I tried not to think about Nathan, back at the cave. As far as he knew, I was at Gibson Station by now, organizing a rescue party. He probably expected help to arrive first thing in the morning. I had let him down.

As I rode on, Joey became increasingly restless, shifting around inside my shirt and making the spinifex tips under my skin itch. I had to stop and settle him down. I knew he was getting thirsty. I was thirsty too, but we didn't have any water. There was nothing to do but continue riding.

The desert began to change. Towards midnight, I felt safe enough to switch the Kawasaki's headlight back on. It lit up a wide red plain scattered with saltbush. The ghostly white shrubs looked like sheep. Here and there I passed low, scrawny trees. There were no more sand dunes. No more sand. The ground was flat and hard, easier to ride on. I was able to speed up.

But not for long. Without warning, the Kawasaki slowed down. I gave it more throttle. Instead of accelerating, the bike spluttered a couple of times, then its engine cut out completely. I pulled in the clutch and wobbled to a dusty standstill. The headlight was still shining and so were the instrument lights – that meant the battery wasn't dead. I found neutral and pressed the starter button. The engine turned over with a loud, whirring noise, but didn't start. I tried again. Same result. With a sickening feeling in the pit of my stomach, I opened the fuel tank. It was too dark to see in, so I rocked the bike from side to side and listened for the slosh of liquid.

Silence.

I was out of gas.

A motorcycle without gas is about as useless in the middle of a desert as a boat. I wheeled it over to a small desert oak and lay it on the ground under the spindly branches. Ripping up a few clumps of saltbush, I arranged them on top of the Kawasaki so it wouldn't be seen from a helicopter. Then I set off on foot.

I walked for several hours beneath the wide,

starry sky. I kept the moon behind me. It had been behind me when I escaped from the terrorists, so I figured the safest thing to do was keep going in the same direction. I had to get as far away from the terrorists as possible before daylight. Come dawn, they would be out in force, combing the desert for my tracks. I couldn't let them find me. I had to alert the authorities. But how? I was in the middle of the desert. On foot. With no food, no water, and no idea where I was.

"Face it, Fox," I said to myself. "You don't have a chance."

But I wasn't going to give up without a fight. I kept walking.

Finally, at 4:30 a.m., I could go no further. I was exhausted.

I crept under a low tree and dragged some saltbush branches around my tired, aching body. For the first time, I realized how cold it could get in the desert at night. But I was too tired to care. At least Joey seemed warm and snug inside my shirt. Re-positioning the baby kangaroo so I wouldn't crush him in my sleep, I curled up in my hiding place like a hunted animal and closed my eyes.

15

NORTH

A dazzling flare exploded in the sky.

They've found me! I thought, recoiling from the blinding red light.

Then I came fully awake and realized it was just the sun shining through my closed eyelids. I opened them and squinted at my watch. 10:15 a.m. I sat up, annoyed with myself for sleeping so long. I had wasted half the morning. Nathan needed help. And the terrorists' secret training camp had to be reported to the authorities and closed down.

I struggled out of my hiding place and stood up. I was still half-asleep, damp with perspiration and itchy all over. My shoulder felt sore where the dingo had nipped me. Joey made things worse by scratching around inside my shirt. I undid a couple of buttons and lifted him out. Blinking in the bright sunlight, the tiny kangaroo licked one of my fingertips. He wanted a drink.

"Sorry, Joey," I croaked – it was hard to talk because my mouth was so dry. "I don't have anything for you." *Or for me*, I thought, as I remembered the grim truth.

I was lost in the desert. I had no transportation, no water, no food. I was going to die!

Keep a cool head, bro. Nathan's voice seemed to come out of nowhere.

It calmed me. I put Joey back inside my shirt and surveyed the horizon. There wasn't much to see. Everything was red and flat, broken only by a sprinkling of saltbush and the occasional wispy desert oak. The sky was a vast blue dome. There was no sign of the moon, so I didn't know which way I had come last night. If I knew which way I'd come, I would know which way to go. I looked for my footprints, but the baked red clay offered no clues either.

Removing my watch, I held it level with the ground and pointed the twelve in the direction of the sun. Then I traced an imaginary line halfway between the twelve and the hour hand. It was a trick Nathan had taught me to find north. Help lay to the north. If I walked in that direction, sooner or later I would reach a road or a cattle station. Provided I didn't die of dehydration first. Or blunder back into the terrorists' camp.

Nathan's map was still in my back pocket. I unfolded it and lay it on the ground with north on the map lined up with north according to my makeshift compass. But the map didn't help, because I had no idea of my own position.

Drawn on the map in blue ink was a small "X" with the coordinates of the cave scribbled beside it. At least I knew where Nathan was.

And I knew where north was.

I put the map away and set off north. It was my only chance. If I ran into the terrorists along the way, I would figure out how to deal with them. *After all,* I told myself, *I had come up against worse dangers and lived to tell the tale.*

But I had never been lost in a desert before. In the blast-furnace heat of midsummer. Without transportation. Without water. Without a hope.

OFF THE MAP

By early afternoon I was a zombie. My head spun, my tongue felt dry and swollen, my skin was tight with sunburn. I was staggering and reeling; I could hardly walk in a straight line. I felt light-headed, weak, dizzy and disoriented. Spots danced before my eyes. The horizon tipped and swayed before me like a stormy ocean. I couldn't think clearly. Even though I kept turning my watch face towards the sun, I could no longer remember how to figure out where north was.

I began to hallucinate. I saw bushflies as big as terrorist helicopters. I saw clumps of spinifex that became kangaroos and bounced off into the distance. I saw a car that morphed into a boulder, a stick that became a lizard, a sun umbrella that was really a bush. I saw a rippling blue lake that flowed away from me as I staggered towards it, then turned into an upside-down waterfall and streamed up into the sky.

I nearly ran into a tree trunk that stepped in front of me and talked.

"Take it easy, brother," it said.

I wasn't fooled. Tree trunks don't walk, and they certainly don't talk. This one had called me brother. It was Nathan!

"How did you get here?" I whispered, in a voice that felt like steel wool in my throat and sounded like paper rustling.

"On Powderfinger."

That made about as much sense as a walking, talking tree trunk. I was hallucinating. I swiped at the hallucination to make it go away, but knocked its hat off instead.

Hallucinations don't wear hats, I realized. It must be real. A real person. I rubbed the sweat from my eyes and looked again. The person standing before me wasn't Nathan. Whoever it was had curly black hair and skin the color of dark chocolate. He was an Aborigine stockman.

The stockman picked up his hat, turned it around in his long brown fingers and placed it carefully on my head.

"Reckon you need it more than I do," he said.

Then he took me by the elbow and led me over to a tree. At least, that's what I thought it was until we got closer, and it morphed slowly into a camel with a rope around its neck and a saddle on its hump. A water bottle hung from the saddle.

The stockman sat me on the ground in the camel's shadow and helped me take a drink. I drank and drank till I ran out of breath.

"Take it easy," he said, laughing. "You'll make yourself crook."

I lowered the big, damp water bottle and savored what remained in my mouth, swirling it around with my tongue. Already my whole body was responding to the life-giving water. My head stopped spinning, and my vision slowly cleared.

The stockman looked about my age, or maybe a year older. He wore a red checkered shirt, dusty brown jeans and tall leather cowboy boots.

"Name's Garry," he said, holding out his hand. "But most people call me Emu."

I told him my name, and we shook hands like adults.

"Where did you come from?" I asked, looking around and seeing nothing but a hazy sea of silver heat in every direction.

"Over there." Emu pointed vaguely over his shoulder. "Been following your tracks all morning. You're lost, I reckon."

I told him about Nathan's accident and everything that had happened since. Emu listened intently, then asked to see the map. I spread it on the ground and showed him where the cave was. Emu studied it for a moment, then scratched a mark in the clay about two inches below the map's bottom right-hand corner.

"We're here," he said.

My heart fell. It was worse than I'd thought. I had traveled right off the map, ending up roughly two hundred miles southeast of where I was supposed to be.

"What are *you* doing way out here?" I asked Emu.

"Catching camels."

I told him about the camels I had seen the previous night.

"Probably the same mob we've been chasing," Emu said.

My ears pricked up when he said "we." "Are there

others with you?"

"Course. There's four of us and Mr. Woods."

"Where are they?" I asked.

Emu waved a hand at the swimming horizon. "Back at Tilden Bore."

"Is it far?"

He tapped his finger in the dirt, roughly halfway between our position and the edge of the map. "'Bout here," he said. "Mr. Woods has a mobile phone. Reckon you can ride Powderfinger?"

Powderfinger, I realized, was the name of his camel. "Sure," I said, climbing slowly to my feet. I still felt a bit wobbly. "How long will it take us to get there?"

"'Bout three hours." Emu glanced up at the sun and frowned. "Maybe a bit longer with two people. Powderfinger's gotta have a drink first. Can I have my hat back for a minute?"

He placed it upside down on the ground and half-filled the crown with water. Then he held it up so Powderfinger could drink from it. Watching them, I suddenly remembered something. Fumbling my shirt buttons undone, I lifted Joey out. The baby kangaroo was limp in my hands. Its eyes were closed, and the tip of its tiny pink tongue protruded from its half-open mouth.

"Give me some water, quick!"

Emu came over. "Poor little fella."

"He got a bit hot inside my shirt," I said. "I think he's in a coma."

Emu replaced the dripping hat on my head. "Too late for him, Sam," he said softly. "He's dead. Want me to bury him?"

I shook my head. I could hardly trust myself to speak. "I'll do it," I murmured.

The ground was too hard to dig a hole. I had to place Joey in the shade of a saltbush and cover him with a few handfuls of dust and pebbles. I laid some small sticks and shriveled leaves on top.

"Sorry, Joey," I whispered, standing over the tiny grave. There was probably nothing I could have done differently that might have saved the baby kangaroo, but even so, I felt like a murderer. I had killed his mother, and now Joey was dead as well, both because of me.

It was my fault too, that Nathan was lying badly injured at the bottom of a cave two hundred miles away. Could I get help to him in time? Or would he die like the baby kangaroo and its mother? Because of me.

I turned to Emu, waiting silently beside his camel.

"Let's get moving," I said.

CALL OF THE WILD

We rode right through the hottest part of the afternoon. It would have been about a hundred and twenty degrees in the shade – if there was any shade. The sun felt like someone was holding a giant magnifying glass in front of it. I wore Emu's hat to protect my already sunburned face and neck, but Emu was bareheaded. He refused the hat when I offered it back to him. Instead, he removed his shirt and tied it around his head like a hood.

Powderfinger didn't seem bothered by the heat. Nor by the fact that he had two riders. He just kept rocking along with his eyes half-closed and his jaw working like an outfielder chewing gum. (I found out later he was chewing cud. It's stuff from an animal's stomach that they regurgitate and eat for the second time. Gross.)

Some people call camels "ships of the desert." I found out why. They move like ships seesawing over a stormy ocean. Riding one is the pits. You can't get into a rhythm like you can on a horse. You jiggle and pitch and sway in every direction. All I could do was hang on, grit my teeth, and pray that the ride would be over soon.

It wasn't.

Powderfinger's saddle didn't make things any better. It had a rickety, wooden frame that dug into the small of my back and knocked painfully against my shins with every step the camel took. The seat was made of old sackcloth stuffed with straw. The straw poked through in about a hundred places and jabbed me through my jeans. It was a one-person saddle. The frame rose up in two tall, A-shaped sections that fit over the peak of Powderfinger's hump, one in front, the other behind, with the padded bit in the middle. There was a fifteen-inch gap between the frame sections – enough room for one person, not enough for two. Emu and I were jammed in like sardines. It was murder.

We tried various solutions. Emu tried perching on the front A-frame, but he kept bouncing off and either landing on me, or sliding down Powderfinger's neck. He tried standing up in the stirrups to give me more room, but every time we went over a bump (and there were lots), his backside whacked me in the face. I tried sitting behind the saddle and clinging on to the rear A-frame. No good. One bump, and I went sliding down the camel's steep, bony backside and dropped six and a half feet to the ground. Luckily, I landed feet first.

We stopped a few times to drink from the water bottle. Each time we stopped, Powderfinger had to kneel to let us off – front legs first, which nearly tipped us over his head, then back legs, like a seesaw going down. We didn't drink much because we had to make the water last until we reached Tilden Bore. Powderfinger didn't get any. That one drink he had before we set out had to last him the entire journey. It didn't seem to bother him. He was a camel.

"Why's he called Powderfinger?" I asked Emu, during one of our drink stops.

"He belongs to my uncle, and Powderfinger is his favorite band." The stockman grinned. "Me, I like

Hilltop Hoods."

I grinned back. Emu was pretty cool.

I looked forward to our drink stops, not only for the mouthful of water, but because it was such a relief to climb down from Powderfinger's back and stretch my legs. But all the time I stood on the ground enjoying the relief, in the back of my mind there was a niggling itch: Nathan was still lying in the cave, expecting help to arrive at any moment.

And the terrorists were still on the loose. I had to report them to the police.

"Let's get back in the saddle," I said, even though it was the last place in the world I wanted to be.

The terrain changed as we journeyed on. The featureless clay plain where I had first met Emu gradually gave way to low red sand dunes dotted with clumps of straw-colored spinifex. It was much like the country I had come through the night before, only in the heat of daylight, it shimmered like molten lava.

Halfway through the afternoon we came upon some camel tracks. There were about a dozen sets of prints, and they crossed our path at right angles. They looked fresh. Powderfinger turned his head and sniffed the air. Then, with an ear-splitting bellow, he broke into a gallop. Emu shouted at him to stop and pulled desperately on the rope to get us back on course, but the camel paid no attention. He was following the call of the wild.

Camels can really move when they want to. It was a crazy, bumpy, rollercoaster ride. Emu's hat flew off my head, but I couldn't make a grab for it – my arms were wrapped around his middle in a sweaty bear hug, hanging on for my life. Both of us were tossed around like rag dolls. The wooden saddle frame jumped and twisted and creaked beneath us. The water bottle thumped painfully against my right leg. Emu was pulling on the rope and yelling at Powderfinger to stop, but the crazy camel just went faster.

The sun danced and jiggled in the sky. My teeth rattled. I was losing my balance and began tipping sideways. I didn't want to drag Emu with me, so I let go and tried to grab hold of the saddle frame behind me. *Missed!* My hands flailed in the empty air. Next moment, I was flying. Then I was falling. With a splash of red sand, I hit the ground and went somersaulting down the side of a dune.

Everything went black.

18

SAND DUNES, SAND DUNES, SAND DUNES

I lifted my face out of the hot, suffocating sand and spat out a mouthful of grit. Powderfinger and Emu were nowhere in sight. Struggling to my feet, I raced to the top of the dune. I guessed it had been about two minutes since I'd taken my tumble – Emu and Powderfinger were probably a third of a mile away by now. Luckily, my estimation was wrong. They were just over the rise. Emu had abandoned ship seconds after I fell. Dragging on the reins, he was leading the reluctant camel up the slope towards me.

"Powderfinger smelled a lady camel, I reckon," he said cheerfully.

The distraction of his wild relatives was too much;

Powderfinger would no longer go the way he was supposed to. Every time Emu and I tried to remount him, he veered off in the wrong direction. Finally we gave up. Pulling the snorting camel around, Emu began leading him on foot, with me perched up on the saddle like a sheik.

Emu's cowboy boots weren't designed for walking on sand. After a short distance, he stopped and removed them. He threaded them upside down onto the branches of a dead gidgee. They were two-hundred-dollar boots, and he was going to leave them behind.

"Pass them up to me – I'll carry them," I offered.

Emu was busily tying his red-and-black socks around another branch. "Nah," he said casually. "I'll get them on the way back."

Barefoot, Emu was much faster. He led us along at a steady jog. But I wondered how long he could keep it up. I knew from last night how hard it was to run across the dunes. I also knew, thanks to my recent fall, how unbelievably hot the sand was. His feet must have been burning.

"Let me have a turn for a while, Emu," I called.

He half-turned and grinned up at me from inside his red checkered hood. His dark skin glistened with perspiration, and I could see his rib cage heaving in and out.

"I'm a good runner," he puffed. "That's why they call me Emu."

He kept running. I hoped he knew where he was going. To me, the sand dunes all looked the same. Emu didn't even have a watch to tell him where north was. After twenty more minutes, I made him stop. I slid from Powderfinger's saddle and handed Emu the drink bottle. "You're going to kill yourself," I said.

Emu took a small sip, then wiped the sweat out of his eyes. "Your brother might die if we take too long."

"He *will* die if you drop dead from heat exhaustion," I told him.

From then on, we took turns. I would lead Powderfinger and Emu for five or six minutes, then we'd swap. I wasn't as fast as Emu (no *way* was I going to take off my boots!), but at least the stockman's brief spell in the saddle gave him time to rest.

It was hard labor. By mid-afternoon we were swapping places at one- or two-minute intervals. Even Emu had slowed to a walk. Powderfinger still hadn't forgotten the wild camels. Each time we tried to ride him in tandem, the pig-headed animal veered off in the wrong direction. We had no alternative but to continue our exhausting relay – one in the saddle, the other stumbling along in front, holding Powderfinger's rope and leading him along like an oversized dog.

The heat was unbelievable. I didn't know how much longer we could keep it up. We were nearly out of water, and I was starting to see spots again.

Red spots.

There were two of them. The nearer one hung low in the sky, about five hundred yards ahead. The second red spot sat on the shimmery horizon far to our left. They looked real. But they weren't flares, they weren't Min Min lights, and they didn't appear to be moving. I was having a spell in the saddle at the time, so I had a better view of the red spots than Emu did. Not that I expected he would see them – people don't see each other's hallucinations. But as we drew closer, the spots didn't fade or disappear like the other hallucinations I'd seen. They grew larger and more distinct.

"Emu, what's that?"

He shaded his eyes. "Looks like flags."

His eyes were sharper than mine; from the crest of

the next dune, I saw that he was right. The red spots were flags. They were about half a mile apart and hung limp at the top of their poles.

"Are there flags at Tilden Bore?" I asked hopefully.

Emu shook his head. "Might be a different camp."

"I hope whoever it is has a mobile phone."

"Or a two-way radio," Emu added.

We were in for a disappointment. When we reached the first flag, there was no sign of a camp. There was no sign of anything, except the other flag in the distance – and sand dunes, sand dunes, sand dunes, in every direction. It was weird – almost like aliens had landed and planted flags to show they had been here. The barren red landscape even looked a bit like a scene from another planet.

"Let me have another look at the map," Emu said. He spent a minute studying it, then folded it and passed it back up. "Tilden Bore's that way." He pointed slightly to the right of our present course.

I wasn't nearly as confident as Emu as we made our way down the side of the sand dune. How could he possibly know where we were? There were no landmarks anywhere, just the two mysterious red flags that didn't mark anything.

But I was wrong about that – they *did* mark something.

"Look!" Emu cried, two minutes later.

We had just come through a gap between two dunes. This time I was leading, and Emu was in the saddle. Directly ahead, swimming slightly in the heat haze, was the dark rectangle of a building.

"HIT THE DECK!"

Something seemed wrong. As we approached the building, I noticed that the wall facing us was crisscrossed with wooden beams. It looked more like the inside of a wall than the outside. There were no windows, no doors, no roof. Two extra-long beams leaned against it, one at each end, like supports.

Emu pointed over to the left. "There's more over there," he said.

We were clear of the dunes now, at the head of a long, sandy valley. About forty yards to our left stood a second wooden structure, identical to the one in front of us. Beyond it, spaced at regular intervals, were four more. The two farthest away were nearly

98

sideways to us. From that angle, we could see they weren't buildings at all. They were just thin, wall-like structures propped up with wooden beams – billboards of some kind. I didn't know what to make of them. What would anyone be advertising out here?

Emu raised his eyebrows. "Someone's coming," he said. Like his eyes, his ears were better than mine too.

I held my breath and listened. After a few seconds, I heard something. Although very faint, the sound was unmistakable. It was a truck or a four-wheel drive. Coming in our direction.

Please have a phone or a two-way radio, I prayed, straining my eyes into the shimmering heat haze.

The valley before us was roughly four hundred yards wide by about a mile and a quarter long. The engine noise came from the other end. I could see a cloud of red dust rising into the air, but the vehicle itself was lost in the mirage that pooled like a silver lake along the valley floor.

"Can you see anything?" I asked Emu.

He stood up in the stirrups. "Just dust." Then he made Powderfinger kneel and swung nimbly to the ground. "Your turn to ride, Sam."

I shook my head. I'd had enough camel riding for

one day – for a lifetime, actually. "I think I'll walk," I said.

Emu rubbed his backside. "Me too," he said.

There was no longer any need to hurry. The vehicle was coming in our direction. It would reach us soon enough. Leading Powderfinger by his rope, we began walking to meet it.

There was a lot of dust, I thought, *for just one vehicle.*

Over the past few hours I had largely forgotten about the terrorists. The heat, the lack of water, my growing concern for Nathan (who'd been underground for nearly twenty hours by now) had pushed all other thoughts from my mind. But I was about to be reminded.

"Leaping lizards!" gasped Emu. He stopped so suddenly that Powderfinger nearly knocked him over.

"What is it?" I asked, frowning at him.

He didn't say anything, simply pointed.

I shaded my eyes.

Oh my gosh!

There were six of them. Spaced roughly fifty yards apart, they came rumbling towards us in a line that stretched from one side of the valley to the other. All we could see were their turrets, floating above the rippling silver haze like strange, alien spacecraft. The lower parts of them – their massive armored bodies, their caterpillar tracks – were lost in the mirage.

Tanks.

"Quick!" I cried. "Get behind the billboard!"

Heads down, we made a dash for the nearest billboard, dragging Powderfinger behind us. The distance was only thirty yards, but it seemed like three hundred.

"Did they see us?" Emu asked, as we cowered, sweating and puffing, in the billboard's thin shadow.

"I guess we'll find out," I said breathlessly.

Up close, the billboard was small. It was barely large enough to hide a camel. Emu had to wrap both arms around Powderfinger's neck to stop him peering over the top. I leaned against one of the rough wooden beams that propped up the structure and listened to the rumble of the approaching tanks.

"Even if they didn't see us, they'll find us if we stay here," whispered Emu.

"What else can we do?" I asked. I couldn't believe my bad luck. Twice in about eighteen hours I'd blundered into the terrorists' secret training operation. Last night had been bad enough, but this time I'd done it in broad daylight. *Good one, Fox!*

"I guess we could make a run for it," Emu said.

I didn't respond immediately. I was listening to the tanks. Their engine noise had changed from a deep rumble to a quiet hum. Cautiously, I peered around the edge of the billboard. The tanks were eight or nine hundred yards away, still half-submerged in the mirage. Their engines were idling, but they were no longer moving.

"What are they doing?" asked Emu, who couldn't look because he had his hands full keeping Powderfinger under control.

Before I could answer, one of the tanks belched a yellow ball of flame. There was a whistling sound, followed by a loud *crack*. The billboard next to ours shuddered as a spray of wood chips and debris flew out of the back of it.

"Jinglers!" gasped Emu, struggling to keep Powderfinger from bolting. "They're shooting at us!"

"I don't think so," I said. "Unless they're very bad shots." Another tank fired. *Crack!* It hit one of the other billboards.

"What are they shooting at then?" Emu asked.

A third shell came whistling up the valley. This one struck the billboard at the far end, taking out one of its wooden support struts. The whole structure turned sideways, allowing me to see what was on the front of it: a large red circle, surrounded by a series of expanding black circles.

Uh oh! I thought.

Before I had time to explain to Emu what was going on, I saw a yellow cannon-flash from the tank at our end of the line.

"Hit the deck!" I cried.

20

GOING DOWN FIGHTING

Even as the words left my mouth, I knew it was too late.

Ker-rack!

A huge shock wave drove me face down into the sand with the force of a pile driver. All the wind was knocked out of me. I saw stars. For a few seconds I was completely out of it.

Then someone was gripping my arm, roughly shaking me. "Sam? Are you all right?"

Still groggy, I looked up. Emu was crouched next to me. He had lost the shirt from around his head, and his hair stood up in a wild, bushy tangle.

"I thought you said they weren't shooting at us!"

he gasped.

My ears were ringing, and it was hard to hear him. "They're not," I said. "They don't know we're here. It's target practice."

"Target practice?" said Emu, looking confused.

I pointed up at our billboard. "Problem is, we're hiding behind one of the targets."

Six feet above us, a large, splintery hole had been blasted through the wood. It was exactly in line with where Powderfinger had been standing the last time I'd looked. Dreading what I was about to see, I slowly swiveled my eyes sideways. And heaved a big sigh of relief. Instead of a dead camel, all I saw was Powderfinger's saddle. Or what remained of his saddle. It lay upside down in the sand fifteen yards away, among a scatter of spilled straw, broken girth straps and bits of splintered wood.

"What happened to Powderfinger?" I asked.

"The shell knocked his saddle clean off," Emu said. He pointed. Far in the distance, a galloping camel was disappearing over the crest of a sand dune. "Gave him a real scare. I couldn't hold him."

I shook some wood splinters from my hair. "Do you think the terrorists saw him?"

"I reckon," said Emu. "But only after his saddle got blown off. They probably think he's a wild one."

There was another loud *crack* from further down the line of targets, and Emu and I flattened ourselves to the ground. We lay there for a few seconds, our faces only a few inches apart. Emu looked terrified, which was exactly how I felt. What were we going to do? We were hiding behind a target, and six terrorist tanks were firing shells at us! I was all set to leap up and run. But somewhere in my brain, the voice of reason started talking to me.

Keep a cool head, it said, in a voice exactly like Nathan's.

It saved our lives.

When the target next to ours took another direct hit, Emu panicked and started to get up. I would have followed him had it not been for Nathan's advice. Instead of jumping up, I grabbed Emu's shoulder and pulled him down beside me. And not a moment too soon.

Ker-rack!

We were showered with a stinging shrapnel of sawdust and splinters. Above us, exactly where our heads would have been if we'd stood up, was a hole the size of a baseball.

"Thanks," Emu said softly.

"Don't thank me, thank my brother."

"Huh?"

"It's a long story," I said. "Are you okay?"

He nodded. "I guess so. But we've got to get out of here. Let's make a run for it."

"No," I whispered, holding him down. "We've got to stay here, Emu. If we lie flat on the ground, they might keep shooting over us."

"You're crazy," he said. "We can't stay *here*!"

I looked up at the two ragged holes. Emu was right: staying behind the target was crazy. But if we showed ourselves, we'd be targets. It was about a hundred and fifty yards to the top of the nearest sand dune. With six tanks firing at us, we wouldn't stand a chance.

"What do you suggest, then?" I asked. I was completely out of ideas.

Emu opened his mouth to speak, but before he'd gotten a word out ...

Kaboom!

The ground shook, the air vibrated, and the target two along from ours exploded in a blinding yellow flash. Emu and I watched open-mouthed as a massive fist of boiling flame punched two hundred feet into the blue desert sky.

The terrorists were using incendiaries now. Exploding shells. The next one to hit our target would blow us to smithereens.

Emu turned to me. "We'll have to crawl," he whispered.

"What do you mean?" I asked.

He didn't answer. Because he was no longer there.

I shuffled on my belly to the end of the target and looked around. Emu was already thirty feet away, in full view of the tanks, *crawling towards them*!

And he reckoned *I* was crazy!

"Keep low to the ground," he called over his shoulder.

I had no choice but to follow. Actually, I *did* have other choices, but they all involved getting blown up. *If I was going to die*, I thought, *I might as well go down fighting.*

It wasn't going to be much of a fight though. Two unarmed boys against six tanks. No contest. I had only gone about twenty yards when a shell whistled right overhead.

Kaboom!

I felt myself lifted off the ground, then I was bodysurfing across the desert on a rolling red wave of sand. The ride only lasted a second or two, then the wave dumped me in a heap.

I saw stars. I felt like I'd been in a car crash. But at least I was alive and nothing felt broken. Rubbing my eyes and spitting out sand, I started to sit up. Only to find myself flattened again. Not by an explosion this time, but by Emu.

"Sorry about that, Sam," he panted. "But you've got to keep your head down."

I pushed him off me and rolled over. In one direction were the fiercely burning remains of the target that had been our refuge until thirty seconds ago. In the other direction were the six terrorist tanks.

"What difference does it make?" I asked. "We're sitting ducks."

Emu shook his head. "Long as we stay low down, the terrorists can't see us."

I didn't get it. "How can they *not* see us?"

"It's something my uncle taught me for hunting kangaroos," Emu said. He pointed at the tanks. "See how only the top of them pokes up out of the heat

109

haze? If we stay low like hunters, they can't see us."

Finally it made sense. The mirage that lay like silver water across the valley floor was screening us from the terrorists' view. We just had to keep our heads down.

"But why are we going *towards* them, Emu?"

He indicated the sand dunes that surrounded the valley on all sides. "We can't go up there. As soon as we start to climb – boom, boom." He made a firing motion with his finger.

I had to hand it to Emu. He was pretty smart.

"So where *are* we going?" I asked, as we started crawling towards the tanks again.

"There's a creek bed just there." He pointed ahead of us. "See those sticks? We might find a place to hide."

For the first time I noticed two or three scrawny branches poking above the mirage, about forty yards away. They were barely thicker than grass stalks and all but invisible in the shimmering heat haze. How Emu had seen them from all the way back at the target, and how he knew they were growing in a creek bed, was beyond me. But I trusted his bushcraft. His people had lived in this country for thousands of years. They knew how to survive in the desert.

But not even fifty thousand years of accumulated survival skills were any match for twenty-first century military technology.

Off in the distance, a tiny ball of flame belched from the tank on our end of the line. It must have lowered its aim, because instead of flying over our heads, the shell hit the ground several hundred yards short of us and came skimming across the sand like a torpedo. It was traveling too fast for the eye to see. All we saw was its shock wave as it sliced through the mirage in a long silver ripple. Heading straight for us.

A tank shell travels at five thousand feet per second. There wasn't even time to duck our heads.

Whomp!

TNT

A cloud of sand exploded into the air forty yards short of where Emu and I lay. For a few seconds neither of us spoke. Both of us had expected to die. But we were still alive. Terrified, but alive.

Emu broke the stunned silence. "That was close," he breathed.

"They must be able to see us," I said. It made sense, now that I thought about it. Last night the terrorists had used infrared scopes to find me in the dark. Of course they had the technology to see through a heat mirage.

We looked at each other. I think both of us knew what the other was thinking. Emu gave me a tiny nod.

"On the count of three," he said. "One, two, three ..."

"Go!" we both yelled.

If there was a world record for crawling forty yards, I reckon Emu and I shattered it that day. By the time we reached the creek bed, we were flying like greyhounds on our hands and knees across the baked red sand. We tumbled in headfirst. Safe!

But we weren't safe, of course. The terrorists had fired a shell at us. They knew we were there.

Or did they?

The tanks went on firing, but their shells kept whistling overhead and hitting the targets – or what was left of the targets. The high-explosive shells were devastating. None came close to our hiding place though. After two or three minutes, Emu and I realized the terrorists didn't know we were there after all. The shell that had nearly hit us must have been a misfire.

We were safe (or as safe as you can be at the wrong end of a tank firing range), but we were trapped. We couldn't leave the dry creek bed without being seen. We were stuck there until nightfall, which was still three or four hours off.

And then what? I asked myself. How was I going to save Nathan? Would he even be alive in three or four hours?

It seemed hopeless. My brother was two hundred miles away, relying on me to get help. And here I was, pinned down by terrorist cannon fire, as helpless as he was. There was nothing I could do for him. I had to wait for nightfall and hope for a miracle.

First, I had to *survive* until nightfall.

Cautiously, I raised my head and examined the creek bed where we lay. Instead of holding water, it was filled nearly to the top with sand. There was only a twenty-yard section that was deep enough to shield us from the terrorists' view – and even that was barely two feet lower than the surrounding desert. It wasn't a good hiding place. Sooner or later, someone would come to check or replace the targets. They would drive right past the creek bed. They would have to be blind to miss us.

Unless we found some way to camouflage ourselves.

The sticks Emu had seen were the topmost branches of several scrawny shrubs that grew along the empty creek. They didn't have enough leaves to hide a goanna, let alone two humans.

"If we break the branches off all of them," I suggested, "we might be able to make a kind of hide like birdwatchers use."

Emu shook his head. He didn't seem to be listening. He was lifting the stringy lower foliage of one of the bushes. It grew near the top of the creek bank where he and I had come tumbling in, and part of the bank underneath it had collapsed.

"There's a hole here," he showed me. "Get something to dig with, and we'll make it bigger."

Where the bank had partially collapsed there was a little sand cave. It was barely a foot across the opening, but it looked quite deep.

"Won't it all fall on top of us?" I asked doubtfully, remembering the cave-in that had come crashing down on Nathan and me the day before.

"Not if we're careful," Emu said. "The bush's roots should hold the roof up."

It was our only chance. If we could enlarge the hole slightly, both of us might be able to squeeze in. Hopefully, the bush would screen the opening from the terrorists' view if they drove past.

I broke a dead branch off one of the other bushes

and tossed it to Emu. "This any good to dig with?"

"It'll have to do," he said.

He stuck his head and shoulders into the narrow opening and started to work. I positioned myself in the shallow depression behind him and used my hands to shovel the loose sand clear as he pushed it out between his legs. Soon we were both breathing hard and dripping with sweat.

"There's a rock or something," Emu's muffled voice came from inside the hole. He stopped digging and leaned further in. "Ouch! It's hot."

The next moment, he flung something out between his legs. Instinctively I caught it. Emu was right; it *was* hot. But I saw right away that it wasn't a rock. It was a long, cylindrical object, roughly the size of a small fire extinguisher. It was painted dark green and had a point on one end. There was something written on it in white. The letters were badly scratched, as was much of the green paint beneath them, but they were still legible: TNT.

"*Holy guacamole!*" I whispered, too scared to drop it, too scared to *move*.

I was holding a high-explosive cannon shell.

INVASION

Emu backed out of the hole. When he saw the shell in daylight, his eyes widened. "Is that what I think it is?"

I licked the sweat off my upper lip and nodded. "It's the one that came straight at us. It must have misfired. I think it's what made the hole."

"Get rid of it," said Emu, looking as scared as I felt. "Throw it away."

"It might be unstable," I whispered, adjusting my sweaty fingers on the shell's hot metal casing. "If I bump it, it could blow up."

"Do you want me to put it back in the hole?"

"No, we need the hole," I said. A drop of sweat

fell from my chin and landed on the shell. I watched it evaporate. "You keep digging," I whispered. "I'll put the shell down at the other end of the creek."

Provided it doesn't blow up first, I thought.

Cradling the hot shell in my arms like a newborn baby and keeping my head down because of the tanks, I shuffled slowly along the shallow trench on my knees. It was hard not to wobble. Every tiny movement felt like it was going to be my last. The shell's pointed end had a gray metal tip that was cracked slightly, and from the crack came a sharp, strong smell like burning matches. One wrong move, I sensed, and I would be splattered across an acre of desert. But I kept going. I only stopped when I was as far from the hole as it was possible to go without revealing myself to the terrorists. Crouched forward on my elbows and knees, I lay my deadly burden gently on the ground and slowly eased my hands out from underneath.

As I lifted my hands clear, I accidentally brushed the pointed end of the shell with my thumb. The shell rolled half an inch and bumped into my watch. I held my breath.

There was no blinding explosion. The world didn't end.

My every instinct was to get away from the shell as fast as possible. But I couldn't. If I left it as it was, the terrorists might see it as they drove past and stop to investigate. That might lead them to our hiding place. With infinite care, just a trickle at a time, I slowly covered the shell with sand. It took ages.

I was concentrating so hard, I didn't hear the approaching turboprop engines until it was too late to make a dash for cover.

It was too late to do anything other than fall flat on my face in the creek bed.

With a roar so loud it made the ground tremble, a shadow the size of Uluru burst over the rim of the creek bed. Everything went dark as a wall of metal blacked out the whole sky. Two enormous tires nearly took my head off.

Then it was gone. A cyclone of red sand swirled around me as the flying monolith thundered off in the direction of the tanks.

I lay still for a few moments, shocked, deafened and partially stunned. My brain tried to make sense of what had just happened. *An airplane*, I thought. *A huge one.* It had missed me by no more than one or two yards.

It was landing on the tank firing range.

They would blow it to bits!

Then I realized there hadn't been any shooting for several minutes. I had been so busy with the shell I hadn't noticed the absence of cannon fire until now.

Where was the shell? I suddenly thought.

Uh oh! I was lying on it.

Trying not to tremble too much, I took my weight on my forearms and thighs, then slowly lifted myself up. There was no explosion. The shell lay partially buried, a patch of green paint and the letters TNT just visible through a dusting of red sand. I smelled burning matches again and thought I saw a wisp of yellowish smoke rising from its cracked nose cone. Hardly daring to breathe, I worked myself backwards until I was clear of the shell, then turned and crawled flat out back along the creek bed towards Emu. He was waiting for me at the mouth of the enlarged sand cave.

"Thought that plane was going to land right on us!" he said.

I raised my head and peered over the lip of the bank. The tanks had moved to the sides of the valley to make way for the landing airplane. It was seven or eight hundred yards away, slowly turning around. Although it was on the ground, it seemed to float like a ship on the shimmering silver mirage. A ship with wings, propellers and a tall, triangular tail. I recognized it now. It was a C-130 Hercules, a military transport plane.

Six tanks and now a Hercules, I thought incredulously. *Were the terrorists planning an invasion?*

"It said Australian Air Force," Emu whispered, beside me. "On the side of the plane, it said Australian Air Force."

"They must have stolen it," I whispered back.

Or captured it, I thought.

Had the terrorists *already* invaded? Had they taken over the country while I'd been out in the desert?

"Emu, have you heard the news lately?"

"Not since two weeks ago." He frowned. "What's that noise?"

The Hercules was taxiing in our direction. Its four engines were kicking up quite a din. But when I paused to listen carefully, I heard another sound. It was coming from behind us, and it sounded familiar. I turned my head.

"Is the hole big enough?" I asked.

Emu was already scrambling towards it. "Hope so," he said, over his shoulder.

We dived for the sand cave and not a moment too soon. Four sleek, brown-and-green helicopter gunships came swooping over the sand dunes towards us, like giant predatory dragonflies.

SCORPION STING

It was a bit of a squash, but Emu and I managed to squeeze ourselves into the hole. We wriggled in feet first until only our heads poked out. Emu dragged one of the overhanging branches down in front of us so we couldn't be seen. But we could see out through the leaves. And what we saw was frightening.

The helicopters landed about three hundred yards away, in a cloud of swirling sand. Because the creek bank impeded our view, all we could see were their swishing main rotors and the tops of their camouflaged tails.

But the Hercules came closer. It taxied to a standstill less than two hundred yards from the end of the creek bed. We could see it perfectly. Even before its four whistling propellers had stopped turning, the cargo door beneath the C-130's broad, raised tail section gaped slowly open like a giant mouth. It swung to the ground and formed a ramp. Two lines of armed soldiers in combat uniform came pouring out.

"It's an army!" Emu gasped.

"Shhhhh!" I breathed.

One of the terrorists was walking towards us. Judging by his fancy uniform and all his ribbons and medals, I guessed he was a bigwig. Emu pulled the branch further down, and we both held our breath. I tried to formulate a plan. Bigwig wasn't carrying a gun like the other terrorists. All he had was a pistol in a holster. If Emu and I took him by surprise, we might be able to grab his pistol before he did. We could take him hostage. We could get him to tell the other terrorists to drop their guns, then make our getaway in one of the helicopters. The pilot would have to obey us if we had Bigwig as a hostage.

But Bigwig didn't come close enough for us to put my plan into action. He stopped at the end of the creek bed, about fifteen yards from our hiding place. His medals flashed in the late afternoon sun as he turned sideways to us. Another soldier came walking towards him. This one wasn't a bigwig; he looked like a junior officer – probably Bigwig's aide. He carried a small radio telephone. Bigwig took the phone and began speaking into it. We couldn't hear what he was saying because the tanks were arriving. Roaring and clanking like bulldozers, they pulled up in a row next to the Hercules. Hatches popped open, and their crewmen emerged, four from each one. They climbed down and lined up in front of their tanks.

Emu nudged my arm and pointed. A cloud of dust appeared in the distance. Half a minute later, eight large, camouflaged trucks trundled into view. They stopped next to the tanks, and soldiers began jumping out over the tailgates.

While this was going on, three commanding officers from the Hercules had formed the other soldiers into platoons. They marched across the sand and halted fifty yards away, facing Bigwig. The soldiers from the trucks lined up behind them. Bigwig was still on the phone, listening and nodding. The aide pulled a small pair of binoculars from a case on his belt. Raising them to his eyes, he searched the sky somewhere to our right.

"Here they come, sir," he said.

Bigwig ended his phone conversation and barked an order to the troops assembled in front of him. Everyone snapped to attention.

I heard a helicopter approaching. It was just a tiny black dot in the sky. My mouth had gone dry, and I was trembling uncontrollably. The terrorists had gathered here to meet whoever was in that helicopter. It had to be someone important. The terrorist leader, no doubt.

The man who had conquered Australia.

As the helicopter grew in size, I was distracted by a movement to our left. A jeep had appeared from inside the Hercules. It drove down the ramp and came speeding towards us across the sand. It pulled up next to Bigwig, and the driver stepped out.

"Look at the flags," Emu whispered in my ear.

Hanging from a short pole on each of the jeep's front mudguards was a miniature Australian flag.

I wondered what to make of it. If the terrorists had taken over Australia, why were they flying *our* flag?

The helicopter was much larger than the gunships and bigger than the one I'd seen in the terrorists' camp last night. It was a Westland Sea King, with

"Royal Australian Navy" painted on the side. It was true then: The terrorists had captured all the armed forces – the Army, the Air Force and the Navy.

Australia had been taken over.

The Sea King landed in a cloud of dust in the middle of the open space between Bigwig and the troops. As soon as the main rotor had whirred to a stop, a door opened, and two flight crew wearing Navy uniforms jumped out. One of them dropped a folding step into place while the other secured the door. Bigwig snapped to attention and saluted as a uniformed figure appeared in the doorway.

Even from a distance of forty yards, I recognized the newcomer immediately. I had seen him heaps of times in the newspaper and on TV. It was the Air Chief Marshal, who commanded the entire Australian Defense Force. The terrorists must have captured him.

But why was Bigwig saluting him? And why was the chief of the Defense Force saluting back?

Then something clicked in my brain.

The last time I'd seen the Air Chief Marshal was on the television news less than a week ago. He'd been talking about a joint military operation called "Scorpion Sting." It was a training exercise involving all the armed forces, a kind of pretend war that was to take place in the desert.

Suddenly everything made sense. *None of this was real!* These weren't terrorists; they were Australian soldiers. Emu and I must have accidentally stumbled into Operation Scorpion Sting. The shots they had fired at me last night were blanks. They must have thought I was part of their war games. I was wearing a khaki shirt and jungle boots – in the dark I must have looked like a soldier. That explained why nobody had shot at me as I rode away on the motorcycle. That was why there were red warning flags on the sand dunes behind the tank firing range.

Before I had time to tell Emu the good news, a second figure appeared at the helicopter's door.

"Leaping lizards! It's the Prime Minister!" Emu gasped, so loudly that the aide standing next to Bigwig turned and cast a suspicious glance in our direction. As he did, his hand dropped to the grip of the big black pistol on his belt.

Emu and I were fifteen yards from the aide, buried up to our heads in the creek bank, with only a scrawny branch for camouflage. We froze.

For a moment I considered giving myself up. I

wanted to call out, "Don't shoot!" and come crawling out of our hiding place. But would that work? The aide might think we were terrorists. His duty was to protect Bigwig and the Prime Minister and the Air Chief Marshal. To lay down his own life, if necessary, in defense of his superiors. He would probably shoot first and ask questions later.

Only when the aide turned away did I allow myself to breathe again. A fly was buzzing around my eyes, but I couldn't do anything about it. The Prime Minister and Air Chief Marshal were walking towards us. Bigwig and his aide stepped forward to meet them. The Prime Minister shook hands with Bigwig, then all four men came walking towards the jeep, where the driver stood to attention waiting for them. It looked like he was going to drive them somewhere – probably to inspect the troops.

Lying completely still in our hiding place twenty yards from the jeep, I was still trying to figure out what to do. We had to give ourselves up, but now wasn't the time. It would be safer to wait until Bigwig and his important visitors had driven off, then come out with our hands up. That way, we wouldn't be seen as a threat to the Prime Minister, Bigwig and the

Air Chief Marshal; we wouldn't be shot on sight.

It was a good plan, and it might have worked if the Prime Minister had gotten in the door he was supposed to. The driver was holding open the passenger door on the other side of the jeep, but the Prime Minister was so busy talking to Bigwig that he didn't notice. The two men came around the near side of the vehicle, then saw their mistake and stopped.

"Never mind, I'll drive," joked the Prime Minister.

Everyone laughed as he opened the driver's door, pretending he was about to get in. When he swung the door open, the Prime Minister took a small step backwards. And stepped on something in the sand.

I could have yelled out a warning, but nobody would have reacted in time. They would have seen me as the danger, not what was under the Prime Minister's foot, about to explode. From twenty yards away, I could see a tendril of yellow smoke curling up around his ankle.

There was only one thing to do.

24

HERO

Bigwig's aide was the only one who saw me coming. His eyes widened, his fingers fumbled to undo the leather clasp on his pistol holster. The others were still laughing at the Prime Minister's joke. He was holding the jeep's door and saying something about his driver's license being expired.

Twenty yards is a long way to run through heavy sand when a shell's about to explode. And when there's a soldier stepping around the front of the jeep ahead of you, a mean look on his face, pulling a pistol from its holster.

"Get *down*, Prime Minister!" he yelled, bringing his pistol up.

But the aide couldn't shoot because the man he and I were both trying to save was directly between us.

I slammed into the Prime Minister's back doing about eighteen miles per hour. We knocked Bigwig and the Air Chief Marshal over too. The Prime Minister went down like a bag of cement, with me on top of him.

As we hit the ground, there was an ear-splitting boom. I felt a blast of hot air and saw the jeep's door spinning overhead like a frisbee. The entire vehicle tipped up onto its side, then rolled slowly onto its back like a mortally wounded dinosaur as the driver and the aide leapt out of the way. All four tires were flaming.

I must have blacked out then, because my next conscious memory is of an Army medic crouched over me. He had a stethoscope around his neck and a concerned look on his face.

"How do you feel, Sam?" he asked.

I didn't even wonder how he knew my name. "Got a bit of a headache," I muttered.

He asked me to count how many fingers he was holding up (three), then offered me a glass of water. I drained it and asked for a refill. I drained that too, but still felt thirsty. The medic brought me a brimming pitcher.

I was lying on a stretcher in the shade of the Hercules. A group of soldiers stood in a huddle about ten yards away. I recognized Bigwig and his aide talking to Emu. Bigwig had a bandage around the top of his head and was laughing at something Emu was telling him. Emu was no longer bare-chested, but was decked out in an Air Force shirt, an Army slouch hat and a pair of Navy commando boots. He saw me looking in his direction and winked.

"Is the Prime Minister okay?" I asked the medic.

"He's fine." The medic gave me a wry smile. "Apart from a few bruises from that rugby tackle you put on him."

"Sorry about that."

"Nothing to be sorry about, Sam. I expect he'll want to thank you himself."

Which is exactly what happened. When the medic had checked me over and allowed me to get up from my stretcher, the Prime Minister and the chief of the Australian Defense Force both came and shook my hand. So did Emu and Bigwig, and the aide who had tried to shoot me.

"You saved our lives," the Prime Minister said. "You're quite a hero, Sam. I'm personally going to nominate you for a bravery award."

I didn't feel like a hero, and I didn't really care about getting an award. There was something much more important on my mind.

"Sir," I said to the Air Chief Marshal, "how long would it take one of those helicopters to fly two hundred miles?"

25

LONG STORY

I led the way. It felt like we were the last six people alive in a black, silent world. We all wore helmets. A hundred-foot safety rope connected us, in case one of us slipped. The floor was rocky and uneven. In a couple of places we had to climb down nearly vertical shafts. It would have been slow going, but I had been here roughly twenty-four hours earlier, and I knew what was around the next corner.

When we came to the first rock fall, I wormed my way across ahead of the others. Then I unclipped the safety rope from my belt and crawled cautiously forward on my own.

My flashlight beam played back and forth across

the rubble. At first I saw nothing. I began to panic. Where *was* he?

Had there been another rock fall since I left? Was I too late?

"Nathan?" I whispered, barely trusting myself to speak.

From the darkness to my right there was a shuffling noise, then a low cough. I swung my flashlight around.

"You sure took your time," my brother said, squinting into the light.

I made my way over to him. Nathan was lying on his back, exactly as I had left him. Except this time he was grinning. "What took you so long, bro?"

"Sorry," I said. "I ran into a bit of trouble along the way."

"You always run into trouble," Nathan joked. He weakly raised his head. "Who are these guys?"

"This is Captain Morrison," I said, as the medic set a first aid pack down next to Nathan's shoulder and began taking his pulse. "He's an Army doctor. The lady behind him is Flight Lieutenant April Rickard, who's flying us out of here in a Lockheed C-130 Hercules. Did you know they're twice as fast as helicopters, and that they can land in the desert? All they need is about a thousand yards of clear– "

"Whoa there!" cried Nathan, giving me a time-out sign. "You brought the *Army*?"

"And the Air Force," said Flight Lieutenant Rickard.

"And the Navy," said Midshipman Thoren, who was carrying the stretcher.

Nathan lowered his head and sighed. "You never do things by halves, do you, bro? Next thing, you'll be telling me you brought the Prime Minister."

"He wanted to come," I said, "but he had to go back to Canberra."

"Very funny," said Nathan.

"It's true," said Captain Morrison. "The Prime Minister asked me to pass on his best wishes, Nathan. He also said he hopes you make a quick recovery."

Nathan was silent for a few moments, and his eyes moved slowly from Captain Morrison's face to mine. "Little brother," he whispered softly, "what *have* you been up to?"

"Well," I said, "it's quite a long story ... "

ABOUT THE AUTHOR

Born in New Zealand, Justin D'Ath is one of twelve children. He came to Australia in 1971 to study for the missionary priesthood. After three years, he left the seminary in the dead of night and spent two years roaming Australia on a motorcycle. While doing that he began writing for motorcycle magazines. He published his first novel for adults in 1989. This was followed by numerous award-winning short stories, also for adults. Justin has worked in a sugar mill, on a cattle station, in a mine, on an island, in a laboratory, built cars, picked fruit, driven forklifts and taught writing for twelve years. He wrote his first children's book in 1996. To date he has published twenty-four books. He has two children, two grandchildren, and one dog.

www.justindath.com